Entwined Publishing books by Claudia Ambrose

Falling Leaves
Build You Up
Maybe This Christmas

I0692788

Falling Leaves

MAYBE THIS CHRISTMAS

CLAUDIA AMBROSE

ENTWINED PUBLISHING

Maybe This Christmas
ISBN # 978-1-80250-288-6
©Copyright Claudia Ambrose 2025
Cover Art by Kelly Martin ©Copyright November 2025
Interior text design by Entwined Publishing
Published by Entice, an Entwined Publishing imprint

Published in 2025 by Entwined Publishing, United Kingdom.

Entwined Publishing is a division of Totally Entwined Group Limited.

MAYBE THIS CHRISTMAS

Dedication

For Cooper:
for reigniting the Christmas magic in my life

Acknowledgements

Thank you to everyone who read Build You Up and is
back for a second jaunt in Falling Leaves.
Your kind words mean the world!
I'm also eternally grateful to my husband for backing
my wild ideas, and to my family for showing their
support (even when I'm super awkward about
discussing my writing in real life).
As always, thanks to Barb Curtis for reading through
my messy first drafts.

Chapter One

"You have approximately thirty seconds before I call the biddies."

Caleb groaned. His younger sister had taken up a vigil on the other side of his apartment door.

"I'm fine. Just give me a day or so, and I'll emerge, like a bear after hibernation."

His attempt at a joke went straight over Sabrina's head. "Where should I start? With Mom, or maybe Babs?"

Why couldn't he wallow for a few days? He loved his family, but they could be suffocating. He'd get rid of Sabrina sooner if he put on a happy face.

He hefted himself off the couch. He ran a hand through his hair – in desperate need of a cut – and his face, with his three-day beard quickly turning into something his mother would consider 'unkempt'.

He groaned as he stood up and took the short walk to the front door. A few seconds after he unlocked it, Sabrina pushed her way inside. Immediately, she scrunched up her nose and covered her mouth.

"When was the last time you cleaned this place?" She leaned in for a second sniff. "Or yourself, for that matter?"

He turned away from his little sister. "Since before the kids left."

Olivia, his ex-wife, had requested an extra week with the kids at Christmas this year. They would spend the holidays with her partner's family in Utah. He could hardly refuse her — after all, they were divorced but still co-parented like close friends — but he wasn't prepared for how deeply the loss of his kids over the holidays would affect him.

Last Christmas, they'd been separated, but not divorced yet. They'd still felt like a family. They'd had Christmas at his parents, just like every year since he'd left home for college. There was a finality of it that this would be his experience now.

He was already not quite used to being a parent only some of the time. But knowing the holidays would also be a lonely experience only made it worse.

How many Christmases did he have left when they were this small? Emerson was five, and Poppy was two and a half. Sure, there would be Christmas morning video chats. But it wasn't the same. His kids were his world.

Compounded with the fact that he'd been feeling adrift since returning to Falling Leaves last year, an episode of seasonal depression was hardly unexpected.

"You've gone downhill this fast?"

He sighed and slumped back onto the couch. "The apartment is just so empty." He and Olivia split custody. If he missed his kids, they were never far away, and Olivia and her partner, Ashley, had no problems with him visiting their house about an hour away. But now, he couldn't just hop on a plane. He already felt like a third wheel in their relationship. He said nothing when they left, even though it felt like a piece of his heart was being carved out. Olivia and Ashley would have insisted he come along, and he had to find a life of his own someday.

Sabrina flitted around the apartment, straightening things up. "It's been three days. We're worried about you, Caleb."

He ran a hand down his face. "Who's we? You and the biddies?"

"All of us." Her phone began to chime with text alerts. She pulled it out of her coat pocket and looked at it. "Mom and the biddies are around the corner, waiting for my signal."

He tilted his head back and groaned. "This is not a bank heist."

"No, but it's kind of an intervention." She crossed the room and sat next to him. "You shouldn't stay holed up in this pigsty in the meantime."

Since Sabrina had moved up to the mountain to run Sky House Lodge with her husband, Brandon, Caleb had taken a larger role at the family company, Ellis & Daughter. Winter was the slowest time of the year. They had no jobs lined up until January, so all he wanted to do was hide from the world.

"So, what, I'm supposed to move in with you and Brandon?"

They were the better choice. His older brother Sebastian, his family, and their parents lived in town. It was funny how he and his older brother had fled Falling Leaves, Virginia, as soon as they could, but they'd both ended up back here. As if the mountains had called them both home after they'd had their fun.

In his former life, he'd been an environmental engineer. Yet, while environmentalism was still important to him, it no longer filled him with the passion to make it a career. Construction, on the other hand, did. Perhaps it had been in his veins all along.

"I never said that. You're a grown man missing out on his first Christmas with his kids. You're right to be sad. But you know what Dad says about wallowing."

Caleb couldn't remember the exact phrase but grunted in agreement. Something about lying down to wallow was akin to lying in the mud. Once you got down, you couldn't get up without being caked in crud. Their father was full of half-baked colloquialisms.

"So, what's your point, Sab? To make me feel worse than I already do? Because mission accomplished."

Sabrina paused to reply to her text messages. "I didn't mean to. But me making you face what's bugging you would inevitably bring up some of those pesky emotions Ellis men like to push under the rug."

He lolled his head to the side and glared at her. "You've said your piece. Can I go back to wallowing now? If we agree that it's just until the kids return in January? It's a temporary wallow, not even three weeks. I'll even consent to appear at the twenty-odd family functions you and Mom have planned over the holidays. I'll even check in once a day. Fair?"

Sabrina set her phone down and glared at him. "I had another idea. One that will do a better job at taking your mind off things."

He groaned. "You're becoming more like the biddies every day, I swear."

She gave her brother a not-so-friendly slap on the arm. "Come on, get showered and dressed. Trim up that disaster of a beard, too. We're going out."

"Where to?"

She rose to her feet. "The quicker you get ready, the sooner you'll find out. In the meantime, I'm going to clean up." She grabbed a handful of energy can drinks and crushed them between her hands one by one before she tossed them into the trash.

Caleb didn't have it in him to fight anymore. He slipped past his sister toward the bathroom. On the way, he passed the empty room his daughters shared. He exhaled. Maybe Sabrina was right.

* * * *

Emma refused to cry, especially not over a stupid job.

After all, why should she? She hated this job and was going to leave anyway. In January, probably.

Maybe.

Still, as she looked over the workspace she'd occupied for the last three years, she felt a sense of sadness. This was one chapter of her life over. She'd assumed she'd leave by choice, not via a lay-off.

She gave a half-hearted wave to her former boss on her way out. She didn't miss the silent presence of a security guard behind her. Since she was no longer an employee, she must be regarded with suspicion.

How humiliating.

She walked wordlessly to the elevator, carrying a box of various knick-knacks and office supplies she had collected over the years. When the elevator doors opened on the ground floor, she found a mostly empty lobby.

Of course, her manager had waited until after six p.m. to lay her off. A blessing she'd stayed later for once, he'd told her. At least she could start the weekend free, along with her one-month severance package.

She stepped out into the blustery December evening. The last thing she felt like doing was carting her belongings on the Metro.

With a sigh, she nestled the box between her hip and the wall, pulled on her gloves and hat, and tucked the box against her as she began her four-block walk to the station.

Washington, DC, was illuminated for Christmas. White lights twinkled on tree branches, and elaborate decorations hung in the shop windows she passed. She usually loved the holidays. Well, she hadn't always. Now, she could create her own happiness, unlike when she was a kid.

The light changed, and she stepped into the street. She made it no more than three steps before a white Mercedes G-Wagon stopped before her. She cursed under her breath and jumped back onto the curb. The driver flicked the hazards on and swung open the door.

"Emma, get in the car." She looked up to find her fiancé, Davis.

Former fiancé? Current fiancé? She supposed it was the latter, since they'd never made the break official. Their relationship status was nebulous, at best. She still wore the ring because he got mad if she didn't. But they'd had a big fight a couple of months back, and things had never been the same. Neither of them had wanted to make the break official just yet, either.

Out of habit, she'd texted him after receiving the news. He hadn't replied, of course. He was a financial consultant and was always in meetings. Besides, she was well aware of her ranking on his list of priorities.

He made no effort to pretend otherwise. Work was the most important factor in his life. Especially given that his new promotion meant he'd be moving to New York in the new year. They were mostly roommates now, leaving messages for each other on the fridge or occasionally sending a text.

They each got something out of the relationship. She was his glorified assistant, helping to keep his busy life on track. She got to be a bystander in his very fancy life and the security of a stable relationship. Sure, she contributed financially to their life, but she could've never afforded to go fifty-fifty on a life that would suit Davis' standards.

He stepped out of the car, took the box from her, and set it in the backseat. She looked left and right before she ducked into the street to climb in the passenger side. "Sorry. You always told me I shouldn't get into cars with strangers."

He snickered as she closed the door and buckled in. "I know, I know. You tell me a white G-wagon is a dime a dozen in this city. You won't have to worry about that when we move to New York. I'm going to sell the car."

He flicked off the hazards and merged back into traffic along K Street when an opening occurred.

Davis was perfect on paper. Handsome — sure, in a slightly evil young President Snow from *The Hunger Games* kind of way, but whatever — and while not exactly the kindest person in the world, he'd always been loyal to Emma.

As far as she knew, anyway — she never pressed. That was the thing in their relationship — they were both excellent at sticking their heads in the sand.

She exhaled and rested her head against the window. "That's a surprise. You love this car."

They came to a red light and eased to a stop. Davis placed his hand on her knee. "I'm sorry you were laid off, Em, but it works out better this way, doesn't it? Now you can help plan the next chapter of our lives together. You were going to leave at the end of January anyway. Now you get a severance."

Davis had never actually asked her. He'd just assumed, which was fair enough, since they *were* engaged. Technically. Would he have to ask for the ring back for things to be over, officially?

"Not much of a severance, a month's pay, then I'll be on unemployment if I don't find anything new."

She'd lived in DC most of her adult life. New York had never been her cup of tea. The hustle and bustle was too much for her. DC was just enough — with its lack of skyscrapers in the city center and eclectic architecture.

The light changed, and Davis tapped on the gas. "*And* you won't have to work in New York if you don't want to. You can plan the wedding, then take your time to figure out your next step. Do you want to work? Fine. You want to stay at home, that's fine too."

Emma murmured in agreement. Davis was right in one way. She'd never really loved her job as a government affairs associate. It was only her second job after graduating from college twelve years ago. She'd been stuck for years. Too anxious to leave because it was a well-paying and low-effort job.

Still, Davis believed his dreams should be enough for both of them. When she thought about her life after marriage, her mind went blank. Well, except for the occasional pipe dream. She didn't fit in with the girlfriends of Davis' friends now, and she couldn't see that changing after marriage.

Panic crept up when she thought of being Davis' stay-at-home wife. She knew well enough to know *that* wasn't her dream life. As long as she was with Davis, her passions would have to take a back seat.

At another stoplight, he brushed knuckles against her cheek. "We'll figure it out, sweetie. We always do."

Davis turned on a dull financial podcast, and Emma pulled out her phone. She mindlessly scrolled through her social media feeds until an ad caught her eye.

They didn't have any Christmas plans this year. Davis' family lived in Ottawa, Canada. He wasn't very close with them, so they had no plans to visit over the holidays. And her family — well, she had none to speak of. Christmas could be lonely for Emma. Perhaps a change of scenery was just what she needed.

A treehouse lodge in the Shenandoah Mountains. She scrolled through the ad's carousel of photos, each more charming than the last. A grand A-frame building was surrounded by rope bridges leading to what they called treehouse villas. The scene was festive without being over-the-top. She couldn't remember the last time she'd been excited for Christmas of her own making. It was either going to visit Aniyah or Davis' terrible family. She scrolled down to read more information about the Sky House Lodge.

Part of her even debated bringing it up to him. Maybe she could spend Christmas on her own? Because if they did get married, she'd be stuck doing whatever Davis wanted for the rest of her years.

"Hey, babe? What about going here for Christmas? It's outside Roanoke."

He chanced a glance over as they wove through traffic. "Looks cute. Go ahead and book it, Em. I'll be off after Friday until the end of the year, anyhow."

Well, there may be a chance.

"You're awfully agreeable."

Davis was never 'off' from work. He meant he wouldn't be required to be in the office until after the New Year.

"Well, I'd rather be with you somewhere fun than be stuck in the apartment all Christmas break. So, book it, okay?"

She smiled at her phone. Maybe he pitied her after she had been laid off, but he'd told her to book the trip, so she would do just that.

Perhaps it wasn't too late to save her engagement, after all.

Even if she wasn't completely sold on the idea, she had to try at least.

* * * *

Caleb was relieved to find that their destination was Sabrina and Brandon's home, not their parents'. He'd worried that they'd have pulled up and he'd find cars lined up and down the street. There were none to be found. Sabrina must've called the biddies off.

Once a tattered lady — giving ramshackle a run for its money — it stood proud as the prettiest house on Jackson Street. However, he noted that the emerald-green paint on the shutters would need to be touched up come spring.

It began to flurry as they made their way up the stairs and onto the grand porch. Sabrina's cats, Sarah and Jareth, peered out from between the pink curtains.

Sabrina waved a tag over the door handle, and it popped open. "No key is needed to open the lock, just a fob. We got the idea from the doors at Sky House."

Brandon owned Sky House Lodge & Villas alongside the Westmore Hotel Group. The place had been a dump when they'd bought it. Caleb had helped his sister renovate the place. They still had a long way to go before the whole resort was finished. But his sister and brother-in-law had put their heart and soul into this place, and it showed.

"Dinner's almost ready, so get cleaned up, please," Brandon called from the kitchen.

Without thinking, he turned to run toward the half bath, finding Sabrina fast on his heels. They'd been like this since childhood — they were the closest in age, so everything was a competition.

"Knock it off!" Sabrina elbowed him as she switched on the faucet.

"You're wasting water," Caleb chided.

Their hands danced over one another as they washed up. Brandon appeared in the doorway.

"That's the most energy I've seen out of you since the kids left."

Caleb snatched a towel off the rack and dried his hands. "You two are laying it on a bit thick. What's for dinner?" He stepped to make his move past Brandon.

Brandon sidestepped him, keeping him in place. "Spaghetti and meatballs. The kind with ricotta. Your favorite."

"What are you two buttering me up for?" He eyed his brother-in-law with skepticism.

"Well, not so much buttering you up as giving you a chance to step outside your box a bit." Sabrina gave Caleb a push. "All will be revealed over dinner."

Chapter Two

Caleb nudged his food around on his plate. "Are you going to make me finish every last bite like a little kid before you tell me what's going on?"

Sabrina set a fresh beer in front of him. "We'll tell you now. Anything to knock that dour look off your face."

He edged his chair back from the table. "So, what is it, then?"

Sabrina leaned closer to him. "We're all worried about you, Caleb. Ever since Olivia shared her plans, we knew this Christmas would be hard for you. We don't want you to be alone. You've been stuck in rutsville, my dude. It's time to make your departure."

He knew they were right, but he didn't appreciate the bluntness of their approach.

"Hence the ambush at my place, yes, yes. I'm caught up now."

"Okay, fine. No one wants to see you isolate yourself this Christmas. No jobs are on the docket until the new year, so you won't have an excuse to leave the house. So, there's two options."

He wasn't exactly in the mood for his baby sister and her husband to be bossing him around, but this would end sooner if he let them express their thoughts. Caleb popped the cap on his beer. "Which are?"

"Option number one. Help the biddies with their annual toy drive. Meaning you'll be doing most of the grunt work and standing out on Silver Spring Street in an ill-fitting Santa suit, pestering passersby for donations," Sabrina said.

"You're leading with the worst option."

One of the cats jumped in Sabrina's lap and she began to stroke it under the chin. "Do you remember Avalee?"

He took a sip of his beer. "Should I?"

"She was the activities director at Sky House. She left us under rather...unfortunate circumstances yesterday," Brandon said.

"That sounds ominous. Did she die?"

"No, she was screwing around with her boyfriend in a cabin. Guests caught her. It was a whole thing." Sabrina waved her hand. "Thankfully, she quit before we got a chance to fire her."

"What does that have to do with me?"

Again, he witnessed his sister and her husband exchange glances. He missed that kind of intimacy, when your partner could know what you were thinking with a glance.

"We won't be able to hire anyone permanently until after the new year. So, what's to say you help your local family-owned mountain resort for the holidays?" Sabrina tented her fingers. "After all, you'd be doing us a big favor, helping us out through our first holiday season."

"As the activities director? Have you lost your ever-loving mind?"

Caleb was by far the most introverted of the Ellis siblings. He would rather grind his teeth down with an angle grinder than lead a group of tourists in Christmas carols. Or god knows what else Sabrina and Brandon had cooked up for the holiday season.

"It's not so bad. It's basically acting as a concierge for the guests, arranging their excursions, and keeping up the fun atmosphere at the resort," Sabrina said.

When all Caleb did was stare at her, open-mouthed, in response, she carried on. "Leading the odd tour, running events. You're good at all that stuff."

Oh, wait. They're serious, aren't they?

"I don't know, shivering my ass off in a threadbare Santa suit is looking better and better."

Brandon exhaled. "Look, we both know that the biddies will work you to the bone. This job is pretty cushy. Almost everything is planned out already. You only have to follow the schedule."

"The uniform is far more flattering than hobo Santa," Sabrina added.

He groaned. "I guess deciding to do neither is off the table?"

Sabrina raised her hands. "You know how mom and the biddies are."

He groaned. "Did they offer you membership yet?"

Sabrina's response came in a middle-fingered salute.

They weren't going to let up, he knew that for sure. "Can I sleep on it, at least?"

"Sure. I'll let Mom know you're weighing your options and to leave you alone until she hears otherwise."

"Isn't that a cheery thought?"

Caleb helped them clean up after dinner then made his way home. On his walk home, he wondered again why he'd returned to Falling Leaves. If he'd stayed in North Carolina, he'd probably have landed a permanent teaching job at one of the universities by now. And even if he hadn't, he'd be allowed to wallow in peace.

* * * *

It was well after noon when Emma managed to crawl out of bed. She'd allowed herself one day to grieve her former life. Today was it. Tomorrow, she'd start considering her next steps.

She meandered into the kitchen, finding that Davis had left her one of his infamous sticky notes on the counter. The man's office was a rainbow of sticky notes, coded and placed in a way only he could understand. Emma never went in there for fear of disturbing one.

She peeled the note.

Hey, could you get some boxes from the hardware store? We should start packing for New York.

She placed the note back on the counter and rubbed her thumb over the adhesive to ensure it stayed in place on the quartz countertop. Pulling a container of no-fat, high-protein yogurt from the fridge, she sat in the kitchen nook overlooking the city. After a bite, she pulled a face and added something from the forbidden cabinet.

She kept her store of junk food under the sink with all the cleaning supplies. The last place Davis would look.

After sprinkling chocolate candy on top of the yogurt, she turned back to the window.

It was another gray December day in the nation's capital. Her phone buzzed with a notification. After tapping through the screens, she realized the inquiry she'd sent about booking a cabin at Sky House Lodge & Villas had been responded to.

Hello! Our deluxe tree-line cabin unexpectedly opened from this Thursday, the 13th to New Year's Eve. I can email you the booking information. Just let us know your preferred dates.
Sabrina Ellis-Blake

Part of her wanted to dismiss the message. She could stay in over Christmas and enjoy the delights that the nation's capital had to offer. She could give herself time to decide if she wanted to accompany Davis to New York or not. Movie marathons, perhaps a solo museum trip — it sounded fun.

Also, so typically…Emma. After a day or two, Davis would begin nagging her about the little piles she left in her wake. Books, snack wrappers, a journal, one of the hundred or so pens she had in constant rotation.

If she moved to New York with Davis, her life would be completely different. She'd have to start wedding planning, for one. It should've filled her heart with excitement, finally marrying someone she could rely on.

There should be more to a relationship than that, though? He was reliable, most of the time. But there were no butterflies when she looked at him, not anymore. Probably because half the time he scowled whenever she spoke.

Flashing lights and a stream of police cars and black sedans swept through the street below. A motorcade. She stood at the window until all the vehicles had passed.

Davis had already agreed to the trip in theory. It wouldn't hurt to get more information.

She replied to the DM with her email address and set her phone down. Davis could change his tune once the trip went from hypothetical to reality. But maybe that was its own sign, of a sort.

She was tired of the back and forth, neither of them saying how they truly felt.

Her phone chimed with a video call. It was her sister, Aniyah. She accepted the call. After a moment, Aniyah's face popped up in the center of the screen.

"Hey, nugget. I just wanted to check in with you." She set the phone down. Emma could hear rustling in the background.

"What are you doing?"

"Clearing out the pantry. Thanks to my executive dysfunction, you know I need a distraction to complete tasks."

"Glad I can be of help," Emma deadpanned.

Aniyah's head popped back up. "You know what I mean. I got your text last night after I went to bed. Are you okay?"

Outside of Davis, Aniyah was the only family she had. They called each other sisters, although their bond wasn't born from blood. They'd both ended up in the foster care system. Emma had been somewhat luckier—she'd had a stable upbringing with her grandmother. She was thirteen when Grandma passed away, and Emma entered the system. She had no other living family, with her mother dead and her father MIA.

It'd been a terrible few years for them both, until their final foster home. Those last two years with the Grossmans had taught her what a family could be.

"I'll get through. I always do."

Aniyah's head dipped down again as she began rifling through the contents of her pantry. "Life is more than white knuckling our way through it."

"Did you learn that in therapy this week?"

Her hand flashed in front of the screen, her middle finger raised. "Don't be a smart ass. It's not like you've been to any sessions lately."

"My therapist moved away, remember?"

Aniyah snorted. "I thought they went on maternity leave. You need to get your story straight.

Emma tried and failed not to roll her eyes. "Don't try to make a liar of me."

"All right, so put that on the top of your unemployment to-do list. Find a therapist."

"Okay, okay. I'll work on it."

"I was giving you a hard time, Em. Go back when you're ready. It has been helping me a bit."

"Can we talk about anything other than therapy now?"

"Okay, fine. What's your plan now that you're jobless? I mean, after filing for unemployment. Are you finally going to plan that wedding?"

Davis had proposed well over a year ago. Neither of them had been in a huge hurry to plan a wedding. Davis, because he wasn't exactly sentimental, and his work kept him busy. Emma, because…well. She didn't want to think too hard about her reasoning.

"Why, looking to see what color your maid of honor dress will be?"

A not-so-subtle eye roll told Emma everything Aniyah had to say on the subject. She'd never liked

Davis. However, when pressed, she couldn't nail down exactly *why* that was. She would make some half-hearted excuse about not liking his vibe. That was the thing—he wasn't awful in a way either of them could pinpoint. He didn't cheat or indulge in any vice to excess. On paper, he was perfect.

Ever since they'd had a blow-out argument earlier that autumn, Aniyah didn't bother hiding her disdain for Davis.

"Look, you've heard me say this before. But just because Davis can give you a good life doesn't mean you'll be happy. You're not happy now, why would you be after you two got married?"

Emma glared at Aniyah. "Enough with the therapy talk, seriously. It's my relationship to sort out."

Aniyah let out a sigh. "Fine. You know I'm right, though."

Emma carried on speaking as if she hadn't heard Aniyah. "*Any*way, I think we're going to spend Christmas at a mountain resort in the Blue Ridge Mountains. It'll be nice to get away, don't you think?"

"You could get away and come to Christmas down here. You know you're always welcome."

Aniyah lived with her husband, Kwame, and their two kids. Their family was loud, loving, and occasionally overwhelming. They were all capital E extroverts, and she'd end up hiding in the closet for some solace by the time Christmas came around.

"I know I am. But I'd have to fly. And you know Davis isn't going back to Ottawa for Christmas. So, I'd be leaving him alone."

Aniyah sighed. "So, tell me about the treehouse resort again. I can place my bets on whether he'll agree to go with you."

Emma ignored the sarcasm and told Aniyah everything. By the time their conversation concluded, an email from Sky House Lodge had pinged in her inbox. Maybe it was meant to be.

She spent most of the day rotating between napping and watching trashy reality TV. Around six o'clock, Davis texted her.

Have a mandatory dinner thing with the partners. Will be home late. Did you start packing?

Emma rolled her eyes and tossed her phone face down on the sofa. He was so concerned with packing that he hadn't even asked her to move to New York with him.

Her phone chimed twice more in rapid succession. She softened when she read it.

Sorry, I meant for our trip to the Blue Ridge Mountains. I do have boxes in my trunk for that move, though. I'll bring them up when I come home. Did you get a chance to get any more?

She scrolled down to the final text.

After tomorrow, I'm free. So go ahead and get it booked, Emmybear.

He hadn't called her Emmybear in ages. Clearly, he was making an effort. If a small one. She left her phone on the couch and meandered into her office. Davis' walk-in closet was the sole spot she could call her own in his former bachelor pad.

When they'd first moved in together two years ago, she'd told him that his place had felt like the waiting room of a luxury car dealership. He'd joked that it was just the vibe he'd been going for. He'd promised that she'd be able to make the place her own eventually. Yet every time she'd asked, he'd put her off. Until finally, he'd relented, letting her have the closet.

She flicked on the fairy lights hanging over her desk, which was as opposite from the rest of the apartment as night and day. The desk was painted pale pink, and she'd installed a light white carpet to complement.

Davis had declined her wallpaper choice, so she'd kept the walls white, save a looping pink scroll she'd painted around the perimeter of the office. Every available surface was crammed with jars of pens, paintbrushes, journals, and other ephemera. She flipped open her planner. She flipped through the pages, resisting the urge to grab a pen to cross out all the work events planned for the remainder of December.

Instead, she reached for her art journal. The safe space she had to express her daydreams, fantasies and creativity.

She meandered back into the living room to grab her phone then placed a food order for delivery. Finally, she slipped back into her office — or closet — and closed the door.

She opened her laptop and pulled up an email from Sabrina, one of the owners of Sky House Lodge. Due to the cancellation, they were offering an impressive rate on the cabin, which would likely have been empty otherwise. The cabin was open from this coming weekend until the New Year. She'd included a link to their booking site at the end of the email.

She hesitated. Davis probably intended for them to stay a weekend, maybe three days at most. Her fingers wiggled above the keyboard. She hadn't properly celebrated Christmas in ages. A small flame of happiness lit up within her at the thought of having a magical mountain Christmas.

The time together would help them solidify their plans. It would be good for them.

Oh, what the hell. She clicked the booking link, entered her credit card details, and hit send. She was paying for it, so if Davis didn't want to stay the whole time, that was his choice. And honestly, maybe what they needed. She was tired of the wishy-washy back and forth.

She deserved a little magic, and if she had to find it on her own, so be it.

She snapped a photo of the confirmation and sent it to Davis.

Too late to change your mind now!

She then promptly turned off her phone. She'd deal with him tomorrow.

Chapter Three

"You're doing *what?*" Olivia's face froze on the video call before it snapped back to focus. Her expression was still incredulous. "Caleb, I thought you were just going to chill out at Christmas?"

He'd told Olivia he'd been looking forward to having a break. If he'd told his ex-wife the truth, she would've insisted that he tag along on their trip. It wasn't that he didn't get along with Olivia's fiancée, Ashley. He enjoyed her company immensely. But this was supposed to be a trip for them – *their* new family. He had to accept that his children now had two families. His role in Olivia and Ashley's was limited.

Caleb ran a hand over his jaw. "They need help. Their activities director quit right before Christmas. You know how Sabrina and Brandon are. It's the first year the resort has been open, and they want everything to go perfectly. They need an extra set of hands – it doesn't matter who it is."

She leaned back in her chair and sipped her coffee. It was still early in Park City, but Olivia was never one to sleep in.

"Well, maybe it'll be good for you to step outside your box a little bit. I didn't love the idea of you being holed up in your place until we came home anyway."

"Ugh, I was hoping you'd be the one to try and talk me out of it. I'm not exactly the bright-eyed and bushy-tailed type."

"Well, no, you're not exactly like a cruise director from *The Love Boat.* But that doesn't mean you won't be good at it. It's only for a few weeks, anyhow." Olivia took a long pull from her coffee cup. "Besides, you've been lingering for a while now, Caleb. You should talk to your Dad about the future of the business, especially since he wants to fully retire soon. Do you want to take it over, for good?"

Olivia still knew him better than anyone. There was no point in hiding it from her. "I don't know. You're right, though. I need to make up my mind about my future."

When they'd lived in North Carolina, he'd taught the odd university class here and there. It was fine, but the kids were more concerned with using AI to finish their papers than learning anything.

She let out a laugh. "Yeah, I know. You worked sixty hours a week and barely saw the kids. You seem happier now. But like your life is missing something. You need to give that big brain of yours something to do."

He groaned and stood up, taking his phone with him. "If you even say I'm missing romance, I'm gonna reach through this phone and poke you in the eye."

She laughed. "My dude, you are a romantic at heart. It's not good for you to be by yourself." She leaned closer to the camera. "You know — "

He set the phone face down as he opened the cupboard. "If you're going to tell me you know the perfect person to hook me up with, I'm going to hang up on you. It's too weird, Olivia."

"Turn me right-side up, Caleb."

He did as she'd asked, dropping a coffee pod into the machine. "I wasn't going to say that. I was going to say that it might not be a bad idea for you to do this job to broaden your horizons. And to maybe get used to talking to women that you aren't related to, formerly married to, or are one of the biddies."

He groaned at the mention of the biddies. He'd received a message from Babs Dodge about their toy drive, basically voluntelling him that he'd be participating even though he was working at Sky House. The only upside was that he'd been relieved of Santa duties, which his father would now handle. If there was one thing he didn't miss about living in a small town, it was the biddies — especially now that his sister was starting to meddle like one of them as well.

"So, you're saying I should hunt for women at my sister and brother-in-law's business?"

Olivia groaned. "Stop being willfully obtuse. I just mean that this would be a good opportunity for you to *talk* to people. And women are people. You and I met in college. You had one high school girlfriend before me. You need to get comfortable small talking. Then you can move up to flirting from there."

The coffee machine hissed as it poured coffee into his *Best Dad in the Galaxy* mug. "Okay, fine. You have a point. I'll give it a try. Because we both know my family isn't going to leave me alone either way."

She laughed. "This isn't the hill you want to die on, Caleb."

A sleepy-eyed Ashley appeared behind Olivia. "Not that I've been eavesdropping the entire time, but she's right. It'll do you good."

Olivia leaned back and kissed Ashley on the cheek. "We'll give you a call back later when the kids wake up. Bye, love you!"

The video call ended abruptly. Caleb tapped open the messaging app on his phone and typed a one-handed message to Sabrina.

Fine, you've got me. Tell me when to be there.

* * * *

"All I'm saying is that a weekend away is quite a bit different from over two weeks at a mountain lodge in the middle of nowhere. I barely have one bar, how am I supposed to make calls?"

Emma was only half paying attention to Davis as they rolled up to the resort. The scene before her was straight out of a holiday movie. A large A-framed lodge sat front and center of a circular drive. The lodge was decked out with decorations. Garlands with holly and ribbons wrapped around the wooden posts holding up the expansive carport to the side. Through the picture windows, she saw the hustle and bustle in the lobby. The high-pitched ceilings had to be at least twenty feet tall. A Christmas tree stretched as far as it could toward the roof.

This was the kind of Christmas she'd always dreamed about. Gram had tried her best, but they'd never had much, living on government assistance.

Before Mom died, she'd tried to make Christmas magical for Emma. But she'd had other priorities.

"Emma." Davis' tone was as frosty as the newfound snow clinging to the windshield. "Are you even listening to me?"

She gestured toward the window. "Would you please take a minute to look around you? I'm impressed, and we haven't even gotten out of the car yet."

"You know I'm not exactly a Christmas person."

Oh, Emma knew. She'd hoped to find a new family when she and Davis married. Unfortunately, his family was the type to go on ski trips on the holiday, stopping only to bicker while they got drunk *après-ski* style.

"Well, could you pretend? For me, at least?"

Davis pulled the Mercedes to a stop under the carport. A broad, bearded, blond man decked out in a buffalo-check flannel and khakis knocked on the passenger-side door. He clutched a tablet protected with a festive Christmas case to his chest.

With an aggrieved sigh, Davis pressed a button and the passenger window lowered.

"Why, hello there! You must be the Dale-Parkson party."

Emma clapped her hands together. "We are! And we're so excited to be here."

"We're excited to have you! I'm Brandon Blake. I co-own Sky House Lodge & Villas with my wife, Sabrina. That name is a mouthful—we just call this place the lodge." He reached into his coat pocket and pulled out a red parking pass. "Why don't you hook this on your mirror and park at the Evergreen lot? I'll have one of our bellhops meet you there to take your bags to your treehouse for you while we get you checked in at the lodge."

"Sounds good!"

Davis rolled up the window before Emma could finish her sentence. "He needs to cut back on his coffee intake. It's too early for anyone to be that energetic."

She leaned forward to hook the parking pass on the rearview mirror. "Oh, stop being such a Grinch. This place is magical."

"If you say so," Davis muttered under his breath.

After the bellhop collected their bags, they made their way to the lodge building. Emma extended her gloved hand for Davis to take, but he was too preoccupied with his phone to notice.

She tucked her hand into her coat pocket and tried to shake off Davis' bad attitude. If he couldn't see the magic in a place like this, then this whole trip was just for show. Minimal effort as usual. It was up to her whether she wanted to continue to go along with it.

After all, that was kind of the point of this trip. And so far, the scales weren't exactly tipped toward moving to New York.

But when she thought about what happened after Davis, her mind drew a blank. No job, no place to live. That had to be a terrible reason for staying with someone.

Emma inhaled the scent of evergreen and crisp winter air. She didn't have to have everything figured out right now.

She approached the front entrance, with Davis trailing behind her. Another bellhop whisked the door open for them.

"The front desk is over there, Ms. Dale." He pointed to the far end of the room as if she could miss it. A large oak desk stood proudly under a picture window. Wreaths and garlands wound around the desk.

A tall blonde woman stood behind it. As they approached, a man appeared from behind the counter and spoke animatedly to her.

Not that Emma could make out what he was saying. Her steps slowed as she took in the sight before her. The man wasn't dressed in the flannel and khaki wardrobe like other hotel employees. He wore a pair of faded jeans and a grayish Henley shirt. His dark hair was unruly, haphazard curls sticking out as he brushed it back from his face.

He was...the opposite of Davis in every way. He was dark, broad, and built like a—as cliche as it sounded, given their location—a lumberjack.

"Hello!" the woman called cheerfully. "You must be Emma Dale. I'm Sabrina Ellis-Blake. We emailed earlier this week?"

Emma snapped out of her trance to find that the man was looking at her—no, he was doing more than looking at her. All it took was a glance for her to feel seen, so she quickly averted her gaze.

"Yes, hi. I'm Emma, and this is my fiancé, Davis."

Mr. Tall Dark and Brooding ducked away from the desk with one further look that made her feel as though she was underneath a spotlight. Emma watched him go. Luckily, Davis was still too distracted by a text conversation to notice.

"I've got your keys already. We have your credit card on file. Here's a map of the property." She slid over a glossy, well-designed map. Emma always appreciated design. That and other little things that other people rarely notice.

Sabrina used a red pen to circle the location of their cabin on the map. "You'll go out the back door here and walk to the end of the path. You'll take the first left through the trees, and your cabin will be down the first bridge."

Emma took the map as Davis finally looked up from his phone. "Is there Wi-Fi here? The cell service sucks."

Sabrina cleared her throat before tapping on the map. "The Wi-Fi password is at the bottom of the map here. Although we encourage our guests to unplug and enjoy while they're here."

To that, Davis let out a snort. "Whatever you say."

Sabrina ignored him and handed Emma another sheet. "This is the schedule of events for the week. Things may change, since our events director left us recently. My brother is filling in." She nodded to where the lumberjack stood, flipping through a pile of pamphlets.

Emma forced herself to look away before she was caught.

"So, it should be entertaining either way. Enjoy your stay and let us know if you need anything!"

Emma gathered the keys in her hand and led Davis toward the back door. He took a moment to look around. "I've got to admit, this place is charming. In the 'so sweet it'll give you cavities' sort of way."

Emma looked to her left and found the lumberjack's gaze on her once again. She cleared her throat and grabbed Davis by the crook of the arm. "Come on. Maybe the cabin is made of gingerbread and royal icing."

To that, Davis only scoffed.

* * * *

Sabrina tapped Caleb on the shoulder, making the papers in his hand scatter comically around them.

"What ya lookin' at?" Her voice took on that tone Caleb could only describe as 'annoying little sister'. Not that he would tell her what he was looking at anyway. The pretty, dark-haired guest and her dire fiancé were hardly worth mentioning, especially to Sabrina, whose imagination would run wild.

He turned away from her and began picking up the papers. "I was just looking at the guests heading to their cabin. Anything is better than trying to decipher all this paperwork. Am I supposed to know what all these terms mean?"

Sabrina snatched a paper off the floor. "You mean complicated terms like RSVP or ASAP?"

He grunted as he scooped the papers up and slammed them down on the counter. "It's not too late for me to flee Falling Leaves for Christmas, y'know. I can keep my phone turned off until New Year's."

Sabrina snorted at that. "Look, those were the only guests we have checking in today. So why don't we go through what a typical day on the job looks like? Then, I'll even help you patch up the Santa outfit if you change your mind. I know Babs is probably going to make you work there anyway."

Caleb made a vague gesture with his left hand. Sabrina took that as an invitation and gave him a shove toward the door.

"You start by making sure the signage is out for any events. There's the main board in the lobby" —Sabrina pointed to a handsomely drawn chalkboard —"as well as printing out the dailies and putting them up in various places around the resort."

"And I'm responsible for everything? Including lettering the sign? Because we both know my handwriting is never gonna look like that."

"I'm aware of your limitations. I'll handle the sign." They moved on to the main desk. "Then you'll help set up for breakfast. You'll be in uniform to ensure the guests know you're there to answer any questions they may have. Then the day's activities begin."

"And I have to babysit the guests?"

She rolled her eyes. "A lot of the guests take the shuttle over to the ski resort. Then there are the amenities on site, like the spa. Or they go on their own. We offer activities mostly in the afternoon. Those you'll oversee. But they basically run themselves. You're just there to ensure the instructor shows up and there's refreshments. The schedule is a little heavier now that we're leading up to Christmas. Still, not everyone wants to be go-go-go. So, we need to make sure the guests who aren't joiners are still having fun, too. Strike up a conversation! Suggest an activity when they're feeling up to it! It's all about making every guest have the best experience possible.

"When have you known me to strike up a conversation with a stranger, like, ever?"

Sabrina chuckled. "There's a first time for everything, big brother."

"Cookies with Santa?" He nodded to the chalkboard sign. "Let me guess, I'm Santa?"

Sabrina snorted. "No. That'll be Dad. He's looking forward to it."

"Well, that's one less nightmare to face during these two weeks."

Sabrina chuckled. "Come on, I'll get you a login and show you where the office is. We have some paperwork and training to do before I can let you loose in front of the guests."

Caleb groaned. "The sooner we get started, the sooner it'll be over, right?"

She inclined her head. "The sooner you can get back to staring down one Ms. Emma Dale, sure."

As they walked to the office, he said nothing to his sister. Anything he said would only encourage her, anyway.

But damn, she really didn't miss a thing.

Chapter Four

Since she was not inclined to tour the resort on her own, and Davis had work emails, Emma took one look at their cabin and promptly collapsed onto the bed.

The trip up the mountain had exhausted her. Davis had been on a conference call for half of it, fully ignoring her as usual. For the rest of the trip, he'd moaned about the lack of cell service in the mountains.

She must've needed the rest as it was well after six the next morning when she woke up.

As she slowly came to consciousness, the sound of tapping on a keyboard was the first sound she heard. She groaned and pulled her pillow over her eyes.

"You managed to get connected to Wi-Fi, I see." Emma pulled the pillow off. Davis sat in bed beside her, his laptop screen resting against his long legs.

"Yeah, of course. I figured I'd go through some emails before we got started on this ho-ho-holiday nightmare."

He kept his eyes on the screen. She'd gotten so used to his casual jibes that few of them even registered anymore. But this one hit a little too close to the mark.

"Why the hell did you come if you think it's a holiday nightmare? You could've gone to Canada to spend time with your family. Or wherever they're spending the holiday this year. Vail? St. Moritz?"

He snorted. "They're staying home for once, remember? You and I both know that would be even worse. Mom would be expecting some sort of production, given that we've been together for years now."

By production, he meant a fuss over his proposal. An engagement party, to show them off to all their snobbish friends. It'd been well over a year since they'd visited, so they hadn't seen them since it became official. Though Davis' mother hardly seemed to tolerate Davis, let alone Emma, she still saw them as boxes waiting to be checked off. *Good job? Check. Nice wife? Double check. Children? Triple check.*

Mommy Dearest would be demanding wedding dates or even wanting to plan the wedding for herself in Ottawa. Given that Emma hardly had any family left, she'd say something like, "It just makes sense, dear."

She tossed the blanket off. "Nice to know that you see this trip as a lesser level of hell."

Davis made a start at a protest before Emma stepped into the bathroom and swiftly shut the door behind her.

She gazed at herself in the mirror. Given the unfamiliar space, it took a moment to register the scene. The sage green and white guest towels gave a subtle hint as to where she was. The larger clue was the tasteful Christmas tree tucked into the vanity corner.

She was glad she'd slept through Davis' inevitable tirade about bathroom decor adjacent to the toilet.

She quickly washed her face and then stepped out into the main part of their cabin. Davis was on the phone and hardly noticed her absence.

A traditional Christmas tree sat in the corner of the room, its soft golden lights still twinkling, since they'd forgotten to turn it off the night before.

The lodge had been recently updated, and it showed. The walls were painted in shades of white and green, and they featured unique detailing, creating a subtle tree pattern on the far wall. Her fingers itched to sketch the room in her art journal. She could add a watercolor wash afterward.

Davis would likely chastise her for getting paint on the furniture though, so her journal stayed in her bag.

A small, modern kitchenette stood opposite a walk-out balcony at the rear of the cabin.

She stepped into the kitchen to make herself a cup of coffee before heading toward the balcony. Despite the frigid December temperatures, she needed fresh air. She pulled her robe tightly against her as she tugged the door closed behind her.

The vague, blueish-purple-hued mountains were the backdrop for the scene. Around their cabin were countless others. Some were only steps from the main lodge, and others, like theirs, were only accessible from a series of wooden bridges. Fairy lights were strung along the bridges and rooftops and tossed onto the lower branches of some of the trees.

She took a large inhale, taking in the sharp scent of coffee mixed with the cloud-heavy sky and the nostalgic aroma of pine trees. Her breath spiraled out in front of her.

This place was perfect. That said, she didn't foresee a Christmas miracle. They'd been here less than twenty-four hours. Davis was miserable, and he was making Emma miserable in turn.

She'd been a fool to think otherwise. He'd taken pity on her when he'd told her to book this trip. This break-up was inevitable, and she hated that she was finally facing the music in this picturesque wonderland.

Letting that depressing thought linger, she leaned forward on the railing and took a hearty sip of her coffee.

She wrapped her hands around her mug and exhaled.

The soft *whoosh* of the sliding glass door opening alerted her to Davis' presence. "Hey. I'm sorry for earlier."

She didn't turn. "For which part, exactly?"

There was another *whoosh* – this time of his breath exhaling on a sigh. "Aren't you freezing out here? Can you come inside?"

"In a minute. Let me enjoy a moment of solitude, then we'll talk."

She didn't need to see Davis to know he was staring at her like a fish, desperate for breath. He was accustomed to being the one with the sharp tongue.

He closed the door, and she sipped her coffee quietly, enjoying the sounds of the forest waking up.

* * * *

It was too late to hide from the familiar voices creeping up on Caleb as he helped ready the lodge for breakfast.

Besides, that uniform was too snug to handle all that maneuvering. He worried the seams on his too-tight shirt or khakis would burst. Sabrina had promised to order in a larger size, but with it being Friday, he'd be stuck in the too-tight uniform over the weekend.

"Why, Caleb, don't you look as handsome as the day is long?" Babs Dodge called out. She meant nothing by it—after all, she'd known him since he was in diapers—but Babs seemed to live to make Caleb uncomfortable.

He groaned and continued pulling the dining room chairs down. "You mean not very, right? Considering these are the shortest days of the year."

Babs snorted and poked Inez Munoz in the side. "You always said Caleb was the cleverest of the Ellis children."

"Isn't it time for you two to have a hot flash or something? Leave my son alone." Lainey Ellis rushed up to brush imaginary lint from his flannel. "Is this the biggest size your sister has in stock? It looks a little snug, Bug. You don't want to give old ladies like Babs ideas."

Caleb hated his childhood nickname. Thankfully, everyone else in the family had given it up.

"I can hear that," Babs said. There was no malice in her voice. The biddies—aka Falling Leaves' Coffee & Knitting Society—where very little knitting took place, but gallons of coffee were consumed—had been friends for years. Even the newest members could count their time in the society by years.

"My outfit is fine." He gently moved his mother's hand from his biceps. As if the universe was in on some comical joke, a button popped off, then pinged off the carpet onto his shoe.

"Well, I can sew that on for now. But, Inez, will you go hunt down Sabrina or Brandon? There's got to be some bigger clothes around here somewhere."

"Mom, stop. I already talked to Sabrina about it." Caleb moved away from her to continue pulling chairs down. "What are you doing up here so early, anyhow?" Falling Leaves was nearly forty-five minutes south of the resort, which meant that the biddies had hit the road well before five a.m.

"Get to our age, and you'll find out how easy it is to sleep through the night, Bug."

"Why don't you tag along with Inez and see if you can find Sabrina? I need her anyway. It looks like her morning shift lead is MIA."

To that, his mother rolled her eyes but did as he asked.

Caleb hurriedly finished setting up the dining room before heading into the kitchen to help the staff prepare breakfast.

Luckily, this was a practice he'd done countless times before. He'd be on-site finishing up construction and get roped into helping in various roles around the resort while they worked out the kinks. He didn't mind kitchen work. Why couldn't the manager here quit? He'd be much happier working behind the scenes.

Although Sabrina was easing him into things, the thought of entertaining a group of guests still made him want to barf. He had middle-child issues. Both Sabrina and Sebastian could command a room whenever they wanted.

Caleb would much rather slide into the background. Like right about now, as Inez caught him in her sights.

"I'm busy," he told her as she approached. "Unless you're willing to throw in a helping hand back in the kitchen."

Inez owned The Over Easy Café in downtown Falling Leaves. She used to take on every role from cook to hostess until her kids recently stepped in and took over. Now, she only worked a couple of days a week, meaning her penchant for gossip had increased a hundredfold.

"You can talk while you work." She couldn't help herself as she set serving spoons in front of one of the chafing dishes.

"I can, but I really don't want to."

To that, she snorted. "Tough luck, buddy. I was just sizing you up to see if you'd fit the Santa costume this year." She produced a sewing kit from her purse. "Take your shirt off."

That this was the first person to make this kind of command of him in—well, months—was unsettling, to say the least.

"I'm not taking my shirt off in the middle of the dining room, Babs."

"I can see you're wearing an undershirt. The longer you argue with me, the longer this will take, so come on."

"Fine. But keep your opinions to yourself."

She glanced up at him as he unbuttoned his shirt. He braced himself for some kind of well-meaning fat joke. Sure, his jobs with Ellis & Daughter and at the inn were physical, but he hadn't seen the inside of a gym in a long time. Olivia called him "slightly fluffy" and assured him that *a lot* of women liked that look.

Not her, though. Although, to be fair to her, a lack of mutual attraction hadn't been the cause of their divorce. It was that old cliché — they'd grown apart.

He gestured to the nearby buffet. "You're going to wear this hash-brown casserole as a hat if you start poking at my middle."

Inez chuckled. "I wasn't going to. I do have some tact, you know." She nimbly threaded the needle. "I don't know, maybe it's time to get a new costume this year. The old one is ratty, anyway. Maybe we'll have your mama make you one."

He turned to take a chafing dish from one of the hustling waiters and placed it on the buffet. "Don't encourage her."

The last thing he wanted was to be his mom's next model. Especially since she was still bitter that Sabrina hadn't let her make her wedding dress.

"Hmm, I can see the campaign now. You do have a beard, and it's getting some speckled gray in there."

"May I remind you you've known me since I was born, Inez? Please stop making it weird."

"All right, all right. Here, the button's back on. It should stay put until your bigger uniform gets here."

He wasted no time pulling his shirt back on.

Inez stood. "I'll head into the kitchen to see if they need my help. I might as well get on the payroll anyhow."

She pushed open the kitchen doors. He exhaled when they swung shut after her. He'd worry about his turn at Sexy Santa after he got through the day.

* * * *

Davis was less than thrilled when presented with a list of activities planned for the lodge during their stay.

"Gingerbread house decorating? Are they serious? I thought people bought them ready-made?"

Emma snatched the activity list from his hand. "Come on, let's get breakfast. Surely, you can't find much fault with that?"

Davis' long sigh as he reached for his jacket indicated otherwise. She ignored his sullen presence beside her and tugged her hat over her head as they stepped out of their cabin. While Davis struggled to pull on his leather gloves, she looked around at the other guests approaching the lodge. She stepped off the decking in front of their cabin and onto the bridge leading to the lodge. It swayed ever so slightly in the morning breeze.

Davis' hand on her back nudged her forward. "You know, I keep forgetting to tell you that Evan found this perfect empty storefront in Soho."

With those words, a long-kept dream rekindled from within her. He knew her dream had always been to own and operate a stationery store. The kind where you could purchase a three-dollar pen or luxury letter-pressed invitation suites for the fanciest wedding or gala.

"Oh yeah? I bet the rent is four grand a millisecond in that neighborhood." Besides, it wasn't as if she had officially 'onboarded' — as Davis put it — to their New York move yet, no matter what he might think.

"Yeah, I was thinking it could be a good investment. And if it makes you happy, that's even better."

He pulled her in for a kiss on the forehead. He was trying, but somehow, she knew it was only for his benefit. She exhaled.

"That sounds like an interesting opportunity," she said carefully.

The grand double doors leading into the lodge's main restaurant were in sight. Davis reached for the door. "Sure does. Let's discuss it over breakfast. Do you think they have any vegan options here? Or – "

Davis didn't get a chance to finish as the doors burst open. A German Shepherd puppy scuttled past them, followed by the hunky lumberjack from yesterday.

Chapter Five

Leave it to his mother to neglect to mention that Inez had brought along her new puppy for the trip. The German Shepherd named Daisy—he gathered by the biddies' shouts as she tore toward the back doors—was roughly three months old and fast as a whip. As much as he didn't want to spend the day as the lodge's activities director, hunting for a scared puppy in acres of mountain forest didn't sound much better.

As he barreled past them, Emma Dale's fiancé yanked her to his side.

"Daisy!" he called for her just as she took off down one of the wooden bridges that split off to one of the many treehouse cabins.

"Daisy! Heel!" Caleb's breathless cries fell on deaf ears as the puppy took off toward a cabin. Bent over and gasping for breath, he noticed a pair of feet entering his sight line.

Figuring it was Inez, he ground out an insult under his breath before speaking. "About time you deigned to join me. Where was the puppy all this time?"

"Umm…I was just trying to help."

It was then he noticed the shoes weren't the orthopedic type favored by the biddies. They were those fancy sheepskin boots that Sabrina liked, too.

He jolted upright, finding Emma Dale standing beside him, her fiancé trailing at a distance, before he took a sharp turn to the left.

She looked beautiful in a dark blue coat and a matching hat, a scarf wound around her neck.

"Oh, hi, um…" He couldn't say her name. That would be creepy, right?

"Emma," she said. "Emma Dale. Sorry, it was instinct that had me taking off after you. My grandmother raised hunting dogs."

"Oh, well, you didn't have to do that." Bashful, he brought his hand to his neck. Of course, the first woman to catch his eye since the divorce had a fiancé in tow.

Emma Dale was about five and a half feet tall, with dark hair and the kind of curvy that kept a man warm at night.

"Found her!" a voice called from the other side of the bridge.

Emma managed a smile before heading off toward the voice. Her fiancé came around the corner, his hand firmly on Daisy's collar.

"Turns out she has a recall after all." Something in the way he said it sounded smug.

Emma and this guy just didn't fit. Caleb had barely spoken five words to her, and that was enough to know she was a warm person. The fiancé seemed like he was straight out of an icebox. One filled with finance bros. His vest and buttoned-up shirt gave it away. His older brother Sebastian wore that uniform for years.

"Oh, thank god!" Inez came barreling down the steps. "You found my Daisy!"

She hooked a leash onto her collar while Davis asked her questions about training the dog. Inez's rapidly souring expression told him she did not care for his input.

"Thank you, but she's just twelve weeks old. We're starting obedience school next week."

"Then maybe you should keep a better eye on her until then," the fiancé snapped.

Inez opened her mouth to say something. Thankfully, Brandon appeared and put a hand on her shoulder. "Let's get inside, everyone. We just refreshed the breakfast buffet!"

Inez shot Davis a nasty glare before taking off with Daisy. The other biddies circled her. Caleb knew well enough to know they were talking shit about Davis.

Emma cleared her throat. "Guess we should get back inside. Sorry, we couldn't help more…" She trailed off, looking at him expectedly.

"Oh, sorry. I'm Caleb Ellis. My sister owns Sky House with her husband, Brandon."

"He's our new activities director!" Brandon called helpfully. "You should stop by later this morning to talk to him. We have all sorts of activities planned leading up to Christmas."

Emma pulled a folded-up sheet of paper out of her coat pocket. "I know. I was looking forward to the lunch and learn tomorrow about Appalachian Christmas traditions."

Brandon broke into a broad smile. "Well, we're looking forward to having you!"

Davis muttered something under his breath. Emma shot him a glare, and he plastered on a fake smile. "I'm looking forward to it, too. Whatever I can do to make my girl happy." He placed his hand on the small of her back and led her through the back doors.

Something about the way he said *my girl* irked Caleb.

"See you then, Emma," Caleb called.

She turned, shot him a bashful smile, and ducked her head.

Once she was inside, Brandon ambled down the steps. "Sabrina's theory is that this trip is a last-ditch effort to save their relationship. In case you were...I don't know, curious?"

He glared at Brandon. "I would never mess with a woman who was spoken for. Especially not a guest."

Brandon gestured toward the window. Emma and Davis had taken up residence at one of the tables closest to the window. They were obviously bickering.

"You know this place has a way of bringing people together or pushing them apart."

That was the joke. Brandon and Sabrina had gotten engaged shortly after he'd purchased the place and had grown closer as they renovated it. Several other couples had gotten engaged here. More than a few had broken up.

"Maybe there's something about being in the middle of the woods with limited cell reception and spotty Wi-Fi that has something to do with that," Caleb said.

Brandon shrugged. "Look, it doesn't matter to me much one way or another. I just like seeing the lights turn on behind your eyes, Caleb. It's been a while since I've seen you look at anyone like you look at her."

Caleb winced. Was it that obvious? "Let it drop, please, Brandon. And for the love of god, don't bring your wife into it."

He laughed at that. "We both know Sabrina is a biddie in training regarding her sleuthing skills. I won't say anything, but she'll put two and two together soon enough."

That was what Caleb was afraid of.

* * * *

The maple bacon-stuffed French toast deserved better. Emma stared at her half-eaten plate while Davis tapped away on his phone. The Wi-Fi was better in the lodge than in the cabins, so he was far from the only person reconnecting to the outside world over breakfast.

However, he was the only one ignoring his partner because of her supposed flirting with the activities director. She'd hardly call it that. She'd been helpful and friendly. After all, it was one of the things he'd claimed to love about her. They'd met when she'd helped him find his friend Beau, who had the nickname 'the wandering drunk'. It hadn't been love at first sight or anything, but they'd ended up together soon after.

She pushed her plate to the side and reached for her coffee cup. Before she could bring it to her lips, one of the staff members refilled it for her. When she murmured thanks, Davis looked up.

He reached for his fork to shove a mouthful of hash brown casserole in.

She couldn't imagine spending the next two weeks like this. Nor could she imagine spending the rest of her *life* with someone who seemed to only tolerate her, at best.

"Davis." She cradled her coffee cup between her hands.

"Hmm?" He didn't look up as he scrolled furiously through his phone.

"Davis, I don't think this is going to work."

That caught his attention. "What do you mean? I'm sorry I got jealous when you flirted with the activities director, or whoever he is. But you were making it obvious."

Emma managed a subtle eye roll. "I was being friendly. I wasn't flirting. And that wasn't what I was talking about."

He had the decency to set his phone down. "Then what *are* you talking about?"

She exhaled. "We both know this isn't working, Davis. It hasn't been in a while. I'd hoped maybe we'd come here, and it would reignite our romance. But we've been here less than twenty-four hours. We've been pretty much constantly bickering when you haven't been working."

He narrowed his eyes. "What are you saying, Em? I came here, even though you know it's not my vibe. I wasn't aware I'd have to playact like I was into this sort of thing."

"You don't have to *playact*. But you don't have to act like a dick, either. So, please, I think you should head back to DC."

They sat there in stunned silence. Emma, for having said the words, and Davis, for hearing them.

"What do you mean?" He raised his voice loud enough to be overheard by a nearby table of older women.

With blood roaring through her ears and trembling hands, she slipped the too-fancy engagement ring off and slid it over the table. "Don't act like you're surprised, Davis. Neither of us has been happy for a while. It was foolish of me to think a change of location would change that."

He stared at the ring, mouth agape. She braced herself for a tantrum for the ages.

Instead, he exhaled, his shoulders visibly relaxing. "I'm sorry, Em. I've been preoccupied with this promotion—"

"This has been going on far longer than that," she interrupted. "I don't want things to be horrible between us, Davis. So why don't you go back to DC and focus on getting ready to move to New York? When I get back, I'll pack up my things and help get the condo ready to show."

His mouth opened and closed like a guppy. "Wait, you're serious? You're ending things? And you're staying *here*?"

It was funny—she'd said the words in her mind a thousand times. She figured she'd stutter or struggle to get them out when it came to have the conversation for real.

If anything, she was surer now of her decision.

"Am I the type of person to make jokes like this?"

A storm cloud blew in over his face. He stood so suddenly that his chair toppled to the ground. He stopped only to snatch up the diamond ring before leaving in a huff.

* * * *

Caleb spent the afternoon holed up in Sabrina's office, watching training videos. Despite him being an employee in the loosest terms, he still had to be trained before he could officially work on his own.

Of course, Sabrina and Brandon had filmed the videos themselves, with scripts provided by the Westmore Group. They must've taken some serious liberties because these videos were insane.

"What do we say when a guest propositions us?"

Brandon appeared from behind Sabrina, dressed in a football referee's outfit.

"That's a flag!" He tossed the flag in front of Sabrina. "At Sky House Lodge, we keep things professional."

A knock on the door had Caleb reaching for the remote.

Brandon stuck his head in. "How are you liking the videos?"

Caleb gestured to the screen. "You look ridiculous, I hope you know that."

Brandon chuckled as he shut the door behind him. "It was Sabrina's idea. You know how she is when she gets an idea in her head."

"I do, which is why I still find it surprising you married her."

"Well, you know how love is."

Caleb yawned. "Can I head home now? I promise I'll watch the rest of these videos in my downtime. I need to head to a Santa suit fitting with Mom, and I'd rather get it over with."

"Sure, no problem. You doing okay, otherwise? I know Sabrina strong-armed you into the position."

He didn't want to admit the only exciting thing about the job so far had been Emma Dale's appearance. But now even that was off limits.

"It's better than rotting on my couch, I guess."

"That's an endorsement if I've ever heard one."

As they made their way down to the lobby, they chatted about the packed Christmas schedule both at the lodge and in town. This was the kind of place where no one was left behind, even if you were dragged kicking and screaming into the Christmas spirit.

* * * *

Any trace of Davis was gone when she returned to the cabin. Save the Post-it he'd scribbled and left on the counter.

I'm headed to NYC. When you return to DC, please make arrangements to clear your things. I'm putting the condo on the market the second week of January.
D

She wasn't sure if he had ignored her when she'd told him she'd do pretty much exactly that, or if he was being his usual bossy-ass self.

She let the note flutter from her fingertips to the floor. Somehow, it didn't seem real. They were well and truly over now. And she was stuck here without a ride back to the city.

Or a home or a job to go back to when she got there.

She let out a nervous laugh and walked around the cabin. What had prompted her to do this *now*? Then she thought about how awful it would've been to spend the next two weeks with Davis somewhere he clearly didn't want to be. While she thought Sky House was adorable, it was a far cry from the luxury resorts Davis frequented. Those places were soulless and empty, no matter how much the rooms cost per night.

A tiny part of her had expected to find him waiting for her when she returned. If he'd been there, she wouldn't have apologized…but she would've at least heard him out.

His absence was proof that he might not've said the words, but his feelings were the same as hers.

This relationship had been dead long before they'd arrived in the mountains.

She sat on the edge of the bed and looked around the cabin. Would it be silly of her to stay here until Christmas? She should probably return to the city and plan…whatever she would do with her life.

Another panicked laugh escaped her. She could officially do…anything. Or go anywhere. The thought was freeing and terrifying at the same time.

Her life was hers now, for better or worse.

Moving first in with her grandmother when the rent came due, then from one foster care placement to another, had taught Emma to be careful with her money. She had savings, so it wasn't as if she'd be destitute if she found something by the time those unemployment checks stopped coming.

Emma kicked off her shoes and stared at the ceiling. Starting over at thirty-four sounded terrifying. But it wasn't as though she had a choice. Neither did she know where she'd spend the holidays. What would she do? Return to DC and Davis' condo? Everyone in DC was from somewhere else. She'd likely be among the few in the building from Christmas to New Year.

Alone amongst the remnants of her past life.

No, she had this trip booked, and she'd stay. It was doubtful she'd get much of a refund now, anyway. At least she could figure things out in a new place. Once the holidays were over, the other pieces would fall into place. Hopefully.

But starting tomorrow, she'd be the jolliest little elf this side of the Mississippi.

Chapter Six

Emma jolted to awareness at the sharp ring of her phone. Service was spotty here — she'd already gotten used to holding her phone to the ceiling, hoping to catch service.

Aniyah's name appeared on the screen. Emma sat up and answered the call. Before she could speak, Aniyah said, "Where are you?"

"The treehouse lodge I told you about. In the Blue Ridge Mountains?"

Aniyah chuckled. "You got Davis to go along with that? Wow, I'm surprised."

When Emma didn't reply, Aniyah spoke again. "Are you there?"

"Yeah, I'm here. Davis isn't, though."

The connection remained constant as Emma recounted what transpired since yesterday. Without thinking, she'd mentioned the lumberjack, er...Caleb.

She had to stop calling him that.

"Wait, so you're telling me there's some hot guy that works there who's been giving you the woo-woo eyes, Davis saw and got jealous?"

Emma managed a dry laugh. "Yeah, I wondered if he would pee on me to mark his territory."

Aniyah snorted out a laugh. "Well, you know he's always been insecure. I didn't imagine that would be the thing that had you breaking things off for good."

It was true that even though Davis was handsome and polished, growing up in a cold family that only pointed out his flaws hadn't exactly made him the most secure man in the world. If there was one argument in their relationship, it was over any perceived male attention she received.

"I can't say that it was. I think we both know this was a long time coming."

Aniyah only murmured in response. "So, do you want to come out here for Christmas? We'd love to have you."

Emma's smart watch buzzed with an alarm. The lunch and learn began in fifteen minutes.

"I think I'm going to stay here until Christmas. Maybe a little longer, I don't know. I need a break before I re-enter the real world."

She could hear the smile in Aniyah's voice. "Keep me updated on the lumberjack situation."

Emma groaned. "I ended my engagement less than twenty-four hours ago."

"Em, we both know said engagement has been on life support for a long time. I appreciate that you gave it your best effort, but nobody is surprised by this outcome. Have yourself some fun while you're on this vacation from reality. I'm decreeing that you shall squeeze in all the fun you've missed out on this year, into the last two-ish weeks of the year."

"Okay, okay. But remember, your idea of fun is clubbing in Miami, and mine is less flashy."

"Sounds like you're in the right place for it, then."

She supposed Aniyah was right. She'd expected to feel…something at the dissolution of her engagement. Perhaps the sadness would come once the shock wore off. For now, she only felt numb. Not quite ready to run into another man's arms, but….

"You're thinking about him, aren't you?" Aniyah teased.

"I think our connection is cutting out," Emma lied.

"We both know it's not, but I'll let you lie to me just this once. Have fun and remember not everything has to be forever. You deserve it."

* * * *

After thirty-plus years, Caleb had learned to tune out the biddies' chatter. A skill he'd had to develop for his own sanity. So, it was no surprise when it took a sharp shove at his shoulder to bring his attention to Babs Dodge.

He'd been attempting to get the lunch and learn prepared. According to Sabrina, they usually only got a handful of people at these events, so they set them up in the back bar. It was lovely at any time of the year, with dark wood and brass finishings. Traditional Christmas decorations hung from the stained-glass lighting fixture hanging over the wooden bar.

"Caleb, I know you see me." Babs poked him again.

"I was hoping you'd take the hint and move on, Babs."

She exhaled a sharp laugh at that. "You know me better than that. Listen, I have some hot goss."

He returned to ensure that the video screen behind the bar was in working order for the presentation.

"Setting up for trivia?" Babs asked.

Normally, that was the primary purpose of the video screen. That or bingo. But the speaker for today had requested a screen for their presentation.

"We both know you don't care about that, Babs. Get to the point."

"Okay, fine, ghost of Christmas pain in my ass," she grumbled. "We've had our first breakup of the season. That pretty girl who helped you find Daisy yesterday? Emma? Her fiancé stormed off, ring in hand."

An unfamiliar feeling flushed over him. Heartbreak for the lovely Emma, but oddly a strange glimmer of hope? No, that was stupid. He brushed it to the side before it could settle.

"Hmm," Babs murmured. "I thought you'd find that news interesting."

Thankfully, she wandered off before he could come up with a reply.

He moved over to the back of the room, welcoming guests in as they arrived. Sabrina and Brandon stood on either side of him, not ready to let him go on his own just yet.

"So," Sabrina said between guests, "we were hoping you could spend the night up here for the next few days. Since the day starts so early, you know. Tomorrow's first activity starts at six o'clock with a pre-breakfast fireside chat."

That didn't sound very good to Caleb. "What do people talk about at six in the morning, anyhow?"

"Oh, we have lots of early risers. You'll make sure the fire is roaring, coffee is bountiful, and have the dailies printed out. That way, the guests are aware of what activities we have on offer. We have a few paid excursions planned for tomorrow, so it'll be a great time to encourage people to sign up for those events."

"Who will be staffed by...me, I presume?"

Sabrina chuckled. "No, silly. You must see them off. We've arranged those trips with outside vendors. You need to make sure everything goes according to plan." She parroted the voice she used with his kids.

He groaned. "You're saying you don't want me to wallow at home? So, the solution is getting up at the crack of dawn to upsell your guests?"

Sabrina ignored the jibe. "We were more concerned about you getting here in time, given the weather forecast this week. We want one of us up here just in case the weather turns bad."

The forecast did call for snow over the weekend. "I'll stay, it's no big deal. The drive is long, and I'd rather stay here anyway. Especially with the fireside chats starting at the butt-crack of dawn."

December was the darkest period of the year, so it was dark when he left and dark again well before the day was over. All that trouble to return to an empty apartment was simply a reminder that his girls were gone, and he wouldn't see them until after Christmas.

"Good," Brandon said. "Sabrina packed a duffle for you and left it in one of the staff rooms upstairs."

Caleb could have remarked about the invasion of privacy caused by his younger sister rifling through his underwear drawer, but he let the moment slide.

Mainly because his attention was drawn elsewhere. Emma Dale slipped through the crowd, towards the bar. She wore a buffalo plaid jacket and a white hat that sat back on her head. How was she adorable and sexy all at once?

"Hmm," Sabrina muttered to herself. "Look who's showing up to lunch minus one annoying fiancé."

"Okay, biddie-in-training," Caleb snapped. It was unlikely that Emma's stay would be very long — if she was truly alone.

Emma approached them.

"Hello, Miss Dale," Brandon said. "Are you ready to learn about Appalachian Christmas traditions?"

"The chef has also cooked up an amazing meal," Caleb said.

Emma's gaze turned toward his. Her cheeks were stained pink, probably due to the sub-freezing temperatures outside. A smile reached her eyes. "Yes. I'm starving, so I'm probably more excited for lunch right now."

Caleb cleared his throat. "Can I take your coat?"

He stepped behind her before she could answer. She drew her long brown hair to one side as his hands hovered above her shoulders. He tugged the fabric away and down her arms. A wave of static electricity skittered down her sweater as he moved to hang up the coat.

"Oh, where's a dryer sheet when you need one?" Emma joked as she rubbed her hands down her hair.

Caleb found the perfect place for her coat on the rack.

And an opportunity to fix his face. By the time he'd turned around, the speaker had approached the microphone. Brandon and Sabrina moved forward to show Emma to her seat.

The moment was gone.

* * * *

She was the only singleton at lunch. It was hard not to feel like a loser. Most of the surrounding tables consisted of elderly couples, with the occasional family. They'd even placed her in a booth in the back corner.

Or maybe that was just her being overly sensitive. After all, the Blakes had been nothing but welcoming. And the sexy lumberjack...

Caleb. That was his name. The static electricity at his touch had been a product of the dry air, but she couldn't deny the internal electricity that tingled throughout her body as his fingers had draped down her arms.

It was horrible to say — but she hadn't felt like that in ages. So much so that she'd wondered if she was, at best, complacent or, at worst, just not attracted to Davis anymore. It wasn't as though she tended to find random men attractive. People blurred together for her for the most part.

Somehow, Caleb stood out.

She knew she should be mourning the end of her three-year relationship. It felt like she'd been doing that since Davis had placed the ring on her finger. Besides, it wasn't as if she was jumping into a new relationship or anything. She had a crush on a guy. The kind of silly butterflies in her stomach that usually died before they led to anything serious.

She wouldn't feel guilty about how she felt.

After the presentation concluded, she gazed around the room. A few guests had cornered the presenter in conversation, and most of the others had left.

Caleb stood at the rear of the room, tapping away on a tablet. He looked as out of place as she did. Somehow, he didn't strike her as the holly jolly Christmas type.

He looked up and caught her staring. She quickly jolted from her seat, so fast that it sent an empty glass tumbling to the ground. She groaned as she captured the crowd's attention.

She righted the cup and pulled on her jacket. Her stomach erupted into a flurry of butterflies as he approached.

Again.

But like the coward she was, she sidestepped the group and made a beeline for the side exit.

She'd had enough excitement for one day.

Unfortunately, the message didn't quite reach from her brain to her limbs. Because as she opened the door, she tripped on the threshold and ended up ass over teakettle on the brightly patterned carpet.

Chapter Seven

Caleb was far from the only one who'd noticed Emma's ungraceful tumble. He managed to shield Emma from the gaze of other guests as she righted herself.

"Can I give you a hand?" Caleb extended a hand to her before he could change his mind.

Her hand shot up toward him. He took it without a second thought. He brought his hand to the crook of her elbow and helped guide her to her feet. She winced her eyes shut as he helped her.

"Did everyone see?"

He took the opportunity to notice the smattering of freckles across her nose and cheeks before answering. "No, just me, I think. Everyone else is too preoccupied with the dessert table."

He gestured to where coffee and snacks had been laid out along the bar. The few remaining guests were piling up their plates.

Her eyes snapped open. "I'm not sure if that's better or worse."

He released her hand, unsure of what to make of her comment. "Are you okay? No twisted ankles or fractured wrists?"

Emma snorted. "The carpet has sufficient padding. The only thing hurt is my pride. This seems to be this week's trend, so…I'll live."

He found himself at a loss for words. He wasn't exactly the nurturing type, except when it came to his kids. He was chief boo-boo healer, tantrum calmer…*god, he missed his kids.*

He exhaled and took a step back. She didn't need to know his life story. "I installed the carpet, so I'll take that as a compliment that it was easy to fall on."

She cocked her head. "I thought you were the activities director. You're a jack of all trades, too?"

It was his turn to laugh. "The activities director job is a temporary gig over the holidays. I help run my family's construction and renovation business. I helped renovate this place. You should've seen what it looked like before." He paused. "Well, I can show you." He motioned for Emma to follow him. They exited the hallway and entered the lobby. Off to one side was a collection of photos documenting the renovation.

Emma leaned forward to look. Caleb realized seconds too late that one of the photos featured him and Brandon shirtless on the roof, shoveling off old shingles.

She cleared her throat. "Um, yes, I can see that now." She looked back at him over her shoulder. "Well, since you are the temporary activities director, would you mind showing me what's available for tomorrow and beyond? Since my plans have erm…changed?"

Caleb clasped his hands together. "Oh, you're planning on staying, then?"

She crossed her arms over her chest. "You mean since my fiancé's...ex-fiancé's unceremonious exit? Yeah, I'm staying." She gnawed on her bottom lip. "I don't have anywhere else to go."

Before he could interject, Emma told him that not only had she lost her fiancé, but also her job and place to live.

Toward the end of her tale, she seemed to realize she'd overshared and sputtered to a stop. "I'm so sorry. You didn't need to know all the ins and outs of my personal life. You have your own worries."

Normally, Caleb would've agreed with her. He wasn't the type to show interest in strangers' lives. But he found himself engaged with Emma's plight.

"No, I'm sorry you're having such a shitty holiday season. I kind of am, too, if I'm to be honest."

Emma tilted her head to the side. "You work in a holiday wonderland."

He chuckled. "Not by choice. I was…" He paused. She'd overshared. He might as well. "This is the first Christmas since my divorce has been official. Last year, we were separated, but still together as a family at the holidays. This year, my daughters are with their mom and her fiancée out of state."

Emma's eyes widened. "Oh, that must be so hard. I'm sorry. How old are your kids?"

"Five and two and a half. Poppy and Emerson."

Her face lit up. "Oh, what lovely names! You must really be missing them. I don't know. It makes me feel a little less lonely amongst all the holiday cheer to know I'm not the only one having a crappy Christmas."

Their eyes met. God, she was adorable. But also sexy, with her dark brown curls, brown eyes, and dimples in each cheek.

Oh, crap. He was staring. He cleared his throat. "If you're really going to stay with us through the holidays, we'll work on making your stay the best possible. Starting with dinner tonight."

She blinked her beautiful doe-brown eyes at him. *Ah, shit.* His brain needed a second to catch up with his mouth.

"Dinner? I was planning to get room service and watch a Hallmark movie in my cabin. Is there a special dinner on that wasn't on today's daily list of activities?"

Caleb's brain fired on all cylinders. Normally, he overthought nearly every word that came out of his mouth, especially around a woman as lovely as Emma. Maybe the fatigue of a very long day had him choosing honesty.

Even if he'd just stuck his foot in his mouth. What had happened to what he'd learned in that stupid HR training video?

"No, there isn't. I was suggesting dinner since you're alone and, well, I am too. My sister decided that I would be the overnight staff on duty for the foreseeable future."

Emma shyly looked away. "So, a dinner for strays, then?"

"Sure, if you want to call it that. If any other strays are lingering around, I'll invite them. But in the meantime, would you like to meet in the dining room around seven?"

She still wasn't looking at him. He followed her gaze, toward the grand Christmas tree. An older couple sat in one of the overstuffed leather loveseats facing it, their hands intertwined.

"I'll see you at seven, then." Her dimples deepened as she held eyes for a moment before retreating.

As soon as Emma rounded the corner, the reality of the situation dawned on him. However innocent it seemed, he was having dinner with a guest. He should probably run that by Sabrina and Brandon. Not that he even cared about keeping his 'job' at Sky House, but he didn't want to get on his sister's shitlist.

He needed to catch Sabrina and Brandon before they left for the night. He cast a glance at the busy lobby. Everyone was occupied watching guitar players by the big tree. He squinted and realized it was his father's twin, Uncle Gordon, who seemed to be wrapping up his set.

Shit. If his uncle caught sight of him, he'd be tied up in a conversation for the better part of an hour. He needed to get to the opposite side of the lobby, and fast.

He ducked behind one of the smaller Christmas trees. Then he did his best impression of an Olympic speed walker until he finally reached one of the locked doors leading to the lodge's offices.

He fumbled with his badge at the reader and pushed the door open, nearly colliding into his sister and brother-in-law.

"Whose ass is on fire?" Sabrina asked.

Brandon started to laugh until Sabrina leveled him a look. "Remember that one kid who almost walked into the fireplace last month? This is not a question out of left field."

"And the reason we now have a toddler-proof grate on our extra-large fireplace," Brandon said. "So, I'm sure it's not that."

Caleb let the door shut behind him, forcing Sabrina and Brandon to take several steps back. "Can we talk, please? In private?"

The two of them shared a look Caleb interpreted as *what the fuck?* before Sabrina unlocked her office door, since it was closest.

His sister's type-A personality was on full display in the small space. She'd once had to share an office with their father above their uncle's hardware store. Now everything had a place. He'd probably end up with a label on his ass if he stood in one place long enough.

"What is up, big brother? You're freaking me out a little."

Caleb ran his hands through his hair. "I somehow asked Emma Dale on a date. I didn't mean to, honestly. Well, not a date so much as dinner, since we're both alone—"

"Is that all?" Sabrina reached out and smacked his biceps. "Of course it's not an issue."

"Well..." Brandon started. "As you saw in that ridiculous video, it's not exactly something we encourage. But this isn't *Dirty Dancing*. She isn't Baby to your Johnny."

"And, honestly, I haven't even decided if we're paying you or not for this. We'll have to see if it's in the budget," Sabrina mused.

"You'll be paying me one way or another," Caleb replied.

"All right, all right, knock it off, you two. I swear, every day you make me glad I'm an only child," Brandon said.

"He knows I'm kidding," Sabrina said. "Of course we're paying you."

"So, is it okay? It's just dinner, I promise. She's our only single guest, and I'm up here by myself…"

"Caleb. I think we can trust you to act with integrity. Additionally, it's not uncommon for our staff to share a meal with guests. As long as you're not doing the horizontal mambo while you're on the clock, we're all good," Sabrina said.

He groaned. "I would rather get a prostate exam in front of the whole town than continue this conversation."

Brandon laughed, but Sabrina had a look he liked to refer to as the Lainey — after their mother. Like she was about to start on some self-serving monologue where she reminded him that it was *her* idea that he work here, so he headed toward the door.

"Not a mambo or cha-cha will be seen. It's just dinner."

* * * *

It was just dinner.

Emma stood in front of the mirror, looking at herself for what must've been the tenth time in the last two minutes.

Dinner with a man after you ended your engagement just yesterday!

She shook off the voice. To be fair, she'd dumped him. Sure, she should be sadder that he'd left her here all alone. He hadn't gotten in touch since he'd left, either. Not that it would change anything.

But that was the least of the problems she'd face once this vacation was over.

All the more reason to have fun, before the new year and all those responsibilities settled on her. She thought about calling Aniyah for her thoughts. But she already knew them.

"Only way to get over one man is to get under another!" She did her best impression of her sister's voice, then started laughing.

Not that that's what this was. No. Caleb Ellis was a nice man who'd taken pity on her single self.

A tall, broad, curly-haired man with impressive shoulders, hands...

"Rein it back, Emma. He was being hospitable. After all, this is a hotel." She blinked at herself in the mirror.

She reached for her coat—she'd packed three—a pale pink pea coat that complemented the dress she wore. Dark green, long-sleeved and dotted with teeny-tiny pink reindeer.

Whimsical enough to fly under the radar at dinner with Davis. He liked her whimsy locked up tight—like in her closet office back at his condo.

She finished buttoning her jacket then slipped on a cashmere beret. She shoved her hands into matching gloves and made her way out of her cabin.

The door locked automatically behind her. She took a moment to gaze around her. This place was beyond magical. Snowflakes fell lazily in front of Christmas lights and wind blew through the trees, making the lights dance.

She felt a flutter of something new in the bottom of her belly. Whether she liked it or not, her life was different now.

It was time to embrace it.

Chapter Eight

Brandon and Sabrina had somehow found time to decorate the private dining room before they'd left. Usually serving up to twenty guests, they'd pushed several tables out of the room, dimmed the lights, and lit the table up with flameless candles and a holiday floral display. Along the back wall was one of those built-in gas fireplaces. It wasn't Caleb's taste, usually, but they'd installed a faux stone wall around it.

A far cry from the main dining room, crowded with guests sharing a holiday meal.

To complete the romantic atmosphere, instrumental holiday music flowed through speakers hidden in the ceiling. It'd be a beautiful place to have dinner.

With a girlfriend or a wife. Not a woman he'd met *two days ago.*

He'd texted Sabrina a choice string of words but given that they were making their way down the mountain, they all bounced back with that red exclamation point, claiming they were undeliverable.

Just his luck. God, what had he been thinking, inviting Emma in the first place? She'd just ended her relationship. He'd just started his job here. It was an all-around idiotic idea.

He gazed around the room. Emma really was going to think this was a date. He thought about de-Christmas-ing the room, but it wasn't like he had the time. He closed the door behind him and walked to the bathroom across the hall for what felt like the tenth time since he'd left his cabin.

The nicest clothes he had were his lodge uniform. In a size that fit, finally.

On his way out of the bathroom, he bumped into someone. He caught sight of the dining room uniform — dark blue trousers and a dark green and blue plaid flannel. It was one of the waiters. They'd hired on a lot of college kids home for the season as temporary workers.

Caleb looked up and found the one member of the wait staff with whom he was familiar — Dutch, Sabrina's best friend Eleanor's son. They'd lived with Sabrina until last summer, when Eleanor and Dutch had moved into a farmhouse outside of town. She'd recently retired as Falling Leaves sheriff.

"Yo, Caleb! I heard you're going on a date with one of the guests. Since when can we do that? Because there's a hottie in cabin — "

Caleb clamped a hand over Dutch's mouth and pushed him into the bathroom. At seventeen, Dutch was several inches taller than Caleb. No wonder he was currently weighing which Division One college he wanted to attend on a basketball scholarship in the fall.

"It's not a date. It's dinner. It was supposed to be in the dining room with the rest of the guests, but Sabrina thinks she's funny."

Dutch slapped off Caleb's hand. "You know I wasn't serious? I mean, hell, you can hook up with guests if you want to. If Sabrina thinks that none of us are, well…" He trailed off and held up his hands.

"Don't tell me things I don't want to know, Dutch. Seriously. You know I'm not good under biddie interrogation. Sabrina is well on her way to joining their ranks."

Dutch mimed zipping his lips. "I know how that is. They've been trying to recruit my mom ever since she retired. Now she's playing into their schemes. Your secret is safe if mine is."

"It's not a secret!"

Dutch grinned. "Okay, okay. Call it what you want. Be glad that I'm your waiter tonight. I'll keep things light and fun. Considering you look like a deer about to jump in front of a truck."

God, his anxious energy must be bad if a teenage boy, of all people, was picking up on it.

He groaned and edged past Dutch. "Don't make her uncomfortable. This is just a nice, hospitable gesture."

Dutch headed for one of the stalls. He stuck his head out before he closed it. "Whatever you say, boss."

Caleb groaned as his phone buzzed with a message from Sabrina. Apparently, some of his messages had made it through after all.

Just tell her that a couple had to cancel at the last minute due to the weather. Don't scare her off with one of your gloomy glares.

He groaned. Of course, Sabrina had an answer for everything. She was their mother's child, after all.

He made his way across the hall toward the private dining room. Both doors were closed, although a flickering light could be seen through the frosted glass. He checked the time on his smartwatch. Seven on the dot. He rubbed his hands together. Why was he so nervous? This wasn't even a date, and besides, it wasn't like he hadn't dated since the divorce. He'd gone on three dates in total. Two setups were arranged by the biddies. The last was by Olivia—which was awkward, as he'd imagined it would be. He'd forbidden her from setting him up after that. Once or twice, women he'd met in passing. But he put himself out there on occasion.

So, what was this strange feeling?

As if the universe was in on some divine joke, Emma rounded the corner. She'd come in through the back door, but somehow he'd missed her. Snowflakes clung to her dark hair and jacket. Her cheeks were flushed, and her eyes sparkled.

Well, fuck. So much for keeping this platonic.

"Hi, Caleb," Emma said softly. "It's really starting to come down out there." She took off her gloves and shoved them in her coat pocket. "Are we eating in the dining room?"

He tried to speak, but a boulder had taken up residence in his throat. He coughed into his arm. "Actually, no. We're going to eat in here. Sabrina said that a party canceled at the last minute. She didn't want the room to go to waste."

He pushed open the doors. Emma stood in the doorway, her expression unreadable.

"If it's too weird, we can totally eat in the dining room."

Emma turned toward him. "I'm not weirded out if you're not." She took in his expression. "You kind of look like you are."

He cleared his throat and shifted his weight. "No! Not at all. Well, maybe a little. But it's nothing to do with you and everything to do with Sabrina being pushy."

Emma grinned. "Well, I suppose I should take off my coat then, if we're going to stay?"

Her hands worked on the last button, and she began to shrug off her coat. Caleb came behind her and drew it over her shoulders. His fingers grazed against a tendril of the dark hair at the nape of her neck. She was ice cold.

He pulled her coat off and she turned to face him. In the dim light, he could make out a pattern of reindeer along her dark dress.

"Your dress is adorable," he said. "Not everyone can pull off reindeer."

She pulled at the fabric. "They're subtle—not everyone notices."

Someone coughed behind them. Caleb turned to find Dutch. "Hello, hello! My name is Dutch, and I'll be your server tonight." He focused all his attention on Emma. "Caleb has known me most of my life, so that introduction was for your benefit, Ms. Dale."

She laughed. The kid did have charm—Caleb could give him that.

"Let me take your coat, then I'll be back with a couple of hot toddies, if that's agreeable?"

Emma nodded. "That sounds perfect."

She made her way toward the fireplace at the opposite end of the room. "I'm freezing. Care to warm up by the fire?"

Caleb had been nervous, sweating for at least an hour, but he wouldn't deny her. He had no choice but to follow.

Caleb's cheeks were cherry-apple red. And the fireplace wasn't giving off enough heat for that to be the cause.

He worried his hands over one another while Emma tried and failed to keep her gaze on the blueish-orange flames. Caleb's hands gave up on worrying and he ran one over his beard. A nice, tidily trimmed dark beard, a shade darker than his dark brown hair. Little flecks of silver caught in the fire glow. Aniyah had done a little digging and found his social media profile. He didn't update it much, but through snooping, she'd been able to figure out some basic facts. He was thirty-six. Only two years older than her.

"Hot toddies on the way!" the young waiter called, although he didn't carry the tray himself — another waiter followed him.

"I'm underage, so I have my friend Paul here helping out with the booze."

Paul brought the tray over to them. The glasses had hand-knit cozies, which of course had a Christmas theme.

"My sister's idea," Caleb said. "She got our town's coffee and knitting society to make them."

"The biddies, actually knitting? Who would've thought it?" the young waiter quipped.

Emma blew on her drink. "The biddies?"

"There may be a mayor of Falling Leaves — the town we're all from — but the biddies run things. That dog that nearly took you out yesterday? Owned by one of the biddies."

"They are a force of nature," the waiter said. I've left your customized menus on the table. I'll give you a few minutes to get...acquainted." He waggled his eyebrows.

The glass doors were smoothly pulled shut once again.

"I saw that there's a Christmas tour of Falling Leaves on the list of activities."

Caleb took a sip of his drink. "It's my hometown. As a kid, I hated growing up here because, you know, it cramped my style. But it does have its charms."

Emma wandered over to the table. "Maybe I'll take that tour, then. Are you the tour guide?"

He chuckled to himself. "I suppose I am. I'll have to check with my sister, though."

Emma set her drink down and pulled up the menu. "*Mr. & Mrs. Ellis*. Huh. Was that the couple that had to cancel?"

Caleb started to spit his drink out before he covered his mouth with his hand. He swallowed. "Hmm, I guess so. What a coincidence, given that my last name is Ellis."

Caleb didn't seem to see it as a coincidence, but Emma didn't say as much. She might not be a mind reader, but she knew well enough to know that this setup wasn't his style. If it was, why would he be so damn jumpy?

It was adorable. Maybe it meant that he'd felt the same way she had when they'd first locked eyes yesterday.

She turned her attention back to the menu.

A delicate red-and-white pattern wove around the outside. She ran her finger over the paper. *Nice quality paper weight.*

"Can you see okay? Given the dim lighting, I may have to whip out my glasses."

Glasses? *Oh my.* Caleb was already handsome. Glasses just made him even more so.

"I can see fine. I was admiring the paper weight the menu is on."

Caleb reached into his pocket and pulled out a dark-rimmed pair of glasses. Emma really tried to ignore the funny sort of feeling it gave her.

She failed.

He nudged his glasses up his nose. "Oh yeah? Do you notice little things like that? What do you do for work?"

She set the menu down and returned to her hot toddy. "Well, until a few days ago, I worked as a government affairs associate at a lobbying and law firm in DC." She sipped on her drink. "I compiled reports, read the news, and watched TV. Looking for trends and data that our lobbyists wanted us to track. It wasn't exactly thrilling."

"Oh," Caleb said. "So, what are you going to do now?"

She traced her finger along the rim of the glass. "I honestly have no idea. My life has kind of imploded this week. No job, no fiancé... I guess I can do anything."

He leaned back in his chair. "So, what would you do, if you had the option? Like, if capitalism wasn't a thing."

She chuckled at that. "Well...I've always wanted to open a stationery store. I worked in one for years while attending college. I've always loved paper things." She pointed to the menu. "Like appreciating the font and paper weight your sister chose for the menu."

"Huh," he said.

For a moment, she expected him to be dismissive. After all, it wasn't exactly the kind of typical dream one had.

He reached for his drink. "I actually know a spot in Falling Leaves that would be perfect for a store like that."

Her eyes widened. "Seriously?"

"I mean, not that you're staying in town. I figured you could see it. Maybe it would inspire you to chase that dream, once and for all."

Caleb had shown her more support in ten minutes than Davis had in years. Sure, he'd "encouraged" her to open a stationery business, but she'd always felt that was more of his idea of a potential investment than any real interest in her dreams.

"I would love to see the space," she said quietly. "Although, honestly, I wouldn't know the first place to start with running a business."

"Well, the Ellis family owns several. Sabrina and I work with our dad at our construction business, Ellis & Daughter. She's been spending more time up here on the mountain, though. Helping Brandon run the lodge. This place was his dream, and we all worked together to make it happen."

A spark of hope ignited in Emma.

"My Uncle Gordon and cousin Dennis own the Missing Screw, the hardware store in town. Trust me, if Dennis can keep a business afloat, you should have no problem."

They shared a smile before Dutch burst back into the room. "Are we ready to place our dinner orders, lady and gentleman?" He cast a glance between the two of them. "Or I could come back? It looks like I interrupted something beautiful."

Caleb gave Emma a look that she could only describe as *"Can you believe this guy?"* before snapping up his menu. "Tell your mom it's time to take you to the eye doctor's, Dutch. I'm ready to order."

While Caleb rattled off what he wanted, Emma let out a slow, shaky breath. Somehow, this place seemed perfect—Caleb included. It was best to keep her hopes level to the ground before they got away from her.

However, as she snuck a glance at Caleb, she wondered if it was a little too late for that.

Chapter Nine

Once Dutch *finally* left them alone with their dinner, Caleb relaxed. The kid felt like a jack-in-the-box, just waiting to spring into the room to scare the shit out of him.

Not that it seemed to bother Emma.

He unfurled his napkin. "You know, I have to say you seem rather calm for someone who's had an uncommonly awful couple of days."

To that, she chuckled. "I don't know that I'd call it awful. Honestly, I'm not sure what I was thinking about bringing Davis here. I don't think I would've had the idea if I hadn't been laid off from my job."

"What gave you the idea to come here?" Caleb asked.

"An ad on my social media. This place looked perfect, and I wanted to be anywhere but DC. When Davis agreed to come, it felt like fate. Especially as things hadn't been great between us for a while." She unrolled her napkin and placed the cutlery on the table.

"His departure wasn't exactly unexpected on my end. I just expected it would take a few days before a mysterious 'work thing' came up and he returned to DC."

"Yeah, but he's not coming back, is he?" God, he felt foolish for asking, but he had to. It was all so new, he didn't have a rulebook to follow.

She laughed. "Oh, no. He's not coming back. We're done. I wish he would've told me that before he abandoned me on the other side of the state, but it's fine."

"He won't return to get you when your reservation ends?"

She paused to take a bite of her steak. While she chewed, he wiped his sweaty palms on his napkin.

"No. He may send a car for me or something if he's feeling generous. He essentially informed me that I must vacate his DC condo by the end of next month. There is no coming back from that."

"So, what are you going to do?"

She shrugged. "I don't know, maybe open a stationery store in Falling Leaves? Move back to DC and get another government affairs job? It's terrifying but also kind of not. I can do whatever I want."

Caleb mulled over her words while he cut into his salmon. "Do you have any family in DC?"

Her gaze lowered. "Oh, I'm going to lower the mood with the answer to that question."

"I'm sorry, I didn't mean to bring up a bad memory or anything."

"You didn't. My grandmother raised me until she died when I was thirteen. Mom died long before that— an overdose, if you were curious. Dad, I never knew. When Grandma died, I was put into foster care."

As a reflex, his hand shot out to grab hers. "Oh wow, I'm so sorry."

"It's not a totally terrible story. I did have a couple of iffy placements, but I stayed with Olga and Ben Henderson from the time I was fifteen until I aged out of the system. They were wonderful people. I met my foster sister Aniyah there. We've been best friends since."

Feeling weird for holding her hand for so long, Caleb attempted to release her. Her fingers slipped out and snagged his wrist, holding him in place. "Thank you for your concern. This time of year is hard for me since Ma and Pa Henderson passed. I always wanted one of those big, crazy families, you know?"

He chuckled. "I have one of those. As you can tell, they're kind of overrated."

She moved her hands away. Caleb missed her closeness immediately.

"Do you have other siblings?" Emma asked.

They fell into an easy conversation where Caleb told her about Sebastian, his kids, and how Brandon and Sabrina reconnected. Although this wasn't a date, he felt it was probably time to tell her of his own past.

"I already told you about my ex and daughters."

Dating since the divorce had been tricky. Women were usually split on whether they were interested in dating a man with kids. Some were thrilled at the idea. Others were skeptical, wondering if he was looking for a nanny instead of a girlfriend.

"You did. And now it seems that we're both kind of lonely this Christmas, right?"

It wasn't hard to determine that her thoughts were like his own. This didn't feel like a random dinner to him. But he would let her lead. After all, his divorce had been final for over a year now. Emma's breakup was less than twelve hours old.

"Yeah. We're just two people who've found ourselves solo at Christmas."

They shared a smile. "So, tell me more about your kids."

The awkwardness vanished as Caleb launched into his favorite subject, Emerson and Poppy.

An hour and a half later, Caleb pushed his half-eaten dessert away from him.

"I'm so full I don't think I can move. If we knew each other better, I'd be popping the top button off my jeans open." He grimaced. "Sorry, I didn't mean to make it weird. I'm a little tipsy."

Despite the rather filthy image that flashed across her mind, Emma laughed. "I should've packed some sweatpants for this trip. I'll probably gain ten pounds before I go back to DC."

"Well, we can arrange for you to go into Roanoke to get some if you need it. That's the sort of thing that falls under the umbrella of my job. I think. Anything to keep the guests having a magical mountain experience!" He put on his best fake smile.

"So, I take it you won't be keeping this job after the holidays?"

"No. Winter is always slow for construction, but we have some jobs lined up in town. There's a new bar opening around Valentine's day that we need to do some finishing work on. Then I'm debating applying for a part-time teaching position if one becomes available in the spring."

"Teaching?"

"Yeah, I have a master's degree in environmental engineering. Until I moved home, I taught and tinkered in additional to my day job. I still love it, but, to be honest, I prefer construction. Especially because there are so many opportunities to be environmentally friendly."

"Sounds like you're a busy man."

"Yeah, but I like it that way. I don't do well with idle hands."

Dutch stuck his head inside. "I don't mean to interrupt, but karaoke is starting in the lounge. Mr. Parker — you know the guy who looks like Santa? — is delivering a rounding rendition of Nelly's *Hot in Herre*. I wouldn't want you to miss out."

Caleb and Emma burst into laughter. "I don't think we can miss that. I mean, if you're up for it?" Emma added.

"I don't think I could live with myself if I missed it."

They both groaned as they rose from the table. As they stepped into the hall, a thudding bass led them toward the lounge. The Nelly song ended, to a rousing round of applause.

"Is that…" Caleb craned his neck. "Run DMC?" The familiar strains of *Christmas in Hollis* carried down the hallway. Not exactly the type of song he'd thought would be featured at karaoke.

Without thinking, Caleb drew his arm around Emma's shoulders. "You might find this surprising, but I do know all the words to this song."

"It's not," Emma teased. "You are older than me, right?"

He cocked a brow. "How would you know that, Emma?"

She gave an impish shrug of her shoulders in reply. "I know things. I also might've made use of the Wi-Fi in the lodge earlier."

His arm dropped lower to loop around her waist. "Were you snooping on my social media, Ms. Dale?"

She didn't delve too deeply—that felt creepy and weird—but she'd searched enough to find out that Caleb was only two years older than her. Nearly the identical age difference in her and Davis' relationship.

"Aniyah did most of the digging and reported back. She gave you a tentative thumbs-up."

"Her opinion means a lot, doesn't it?"

She smiled. "More than anyone's."

He dropped his arm to his side as they walked into the lounge. Two of the older women she'd seen snooping around were belting out an off-key rendition of *Jingle Bell Rock*.

"God, Babs and Inez are such a trainwreck. What are they even doing here? Sabrina never told me how much time the biddies spend here." Caleb winced as their off-key rendition began. "Oh god, I think I need another drink. Or two."

"Caleb!" A shrill voice carried over even Babs' and Inez's terrible singing.

He turned to Emma. "I don't want to alarm you, but that woman waving her arms wildly is my mother. If you want to go back to your cabin, I won't think less of you." He had to shout to be heard over the calamity.

Emma leaned in on her tiptoes toward Caleb. "With the rate that woman is hightailing it across the room, I don't think escape is possible. Unless one of the features of this room is a *Mission Impossible*-style escape hatch."

"Unfortunately not, and I would know."

She laughed and leaned in closer to him. God, he smelled amazing.

"All right then, brace for impact."

"Caleb!" The woman barreling toward them stopped suddenly in front of them. "What are you doing here?"

Caleb half-rolled his eyes. "You know why I'm here. What are you doing here? And why are Dad and Uncle Gordon wearing matching Santa suits and cutting a rug? Dad's gonna injure himself again."

Emma's gaze carried over to the far side of the room, where two identical Santas danced in unison to the god-awful karaoke performance. She tuned back into Caleb's conversation with his mother when she felt a tug on her arm.

Emma turned to look at the older woman. Caleb was obviously her son—they shared the same eyes and mouth. Her chestnut-brown hair was pulled up on top of her head, wrapped with a red velvet ribbon.

"Emma Dale. I'm a guest here. Caleb has been keeping me company."

"Oh?" She raised her hand to her face, her diamond wedding ring catching the light.

Emma couldn't help but look down at her empty ring finger. Funny how she hadn't missed the weight of the ring until now, even though she'd rarely taken it off in the year since the engagement. She should miss the weight of it, if nothing else. But she felt lighter, now that it was gone.

"Mom, I think Dad is waving you down. Or it could be Uncle Gordon. They're too far away to tell." He turned to Emma. "My dad and uncle are identical twins."

She waved Caleb off. "They just want me to judge who has the best Santa bellow. If I hear one more *Ho! Ho! Ho!* tonight, I'm going to ho-ho-help myself to an entire bottle of red wine."

Emma laughed. Caleb's family seemed warm and inviting. His mother reached forward to touch her arm. "I'm Lainey Ellis, by the way. Sabrina and Caleb's mom. I'm also Sebastian's mom, but he's not here tonight. He and his wife run Loaved Up, the bakery in town. Have you been to Falling Leaves yet?"

Emma shook her head. "I've only been here a couple of days."

"Well, I'm pretty sure our activities director can give you a tour tomorrow."

"Mom, I have to work."

"Hmm, well, your father and I are staying the night. You get the morning run of activities started, then I'll take over. Emma here really needs to see the town before the storm rolls in tomorrow."

Before he could protest, Lainey wandered off toward Santa and his identical twin.

"I'm sorry. My mom can be a lot."

The off-key duo left the stage, making Caleb's words suddenly loud in the lounge. Several people turned in their direction, including the women stepping off the stage.

"I heard that!" Lainey called from the other side of the room.

Before he could reply, the music kicked up again, with two guests singing *Rudolph the Red-Nosed Reindeer*.

As much as she didn't want this night to end, the throbbing behind her eyes told her she needed to get away from the off-key karaoke.

"I think I'm going to call it a night. Especially if we're going into town tomorrow."

Caleb gently took her by the elbow and led her out of the lounge. "Of course. It's been a while since I've been to karaoke. I forgot how terrible most people are at it." He paused. "I'll walk you back to your cabin."

"You should be glad I wasn't up there. I can't carry a tune in a bucket."

"Me either. The rest of my family has the voices of angels — even my kids. I'm the one on recording duty on holidays."

She laughed. "Your family seems nice."

"Oh, they are. It's just that sometimes I remember when I lived in North Carolina. That distance was nice. But, with my ex and her fiancée living in Blacksburg, it makes sense for me to stay locally."

Despite the raucous party happening in the lounge, the rest of the resort was damn near magical with the Christmas ambience turned up to eleven.

"Sure, of course. It's important to be near your children, I get that."

She'd felt oddly light when Caleb told her he was a father. She loved children, but, given her chaotic upbringing, she'd never wanted children of her own. She'd been content being an auntie to Aniyah's two kids. Davis had never wanted kids either, so it was one thing they'd bonded over early in their relationship.

"You all right? Am I boring you to death? I am drunk and a bit rambly." He pushed open the door leading to the cabins. Cold air smacked them in the face.

"I'm fine. Just a little sleepy." She reached for his arm. "My cabin's just on the other side of the bridge. I can take it from here." She gave his arm a squeeze.

"Thank you for a wonderful evening, Caleb. You helped turn around a terrible week."

The fine lines around his eyes crinkled as he smiled, she noticed. "Oh, you're welcome. I had fun, too." He placed his hand on top of hers. Still warm, despite the cold.

"See you in the morning."

Their eyes locked before she took off toward the bridge. She carefully picked her way across, wary of ice. It took her so long that she'd figured Caleb had returned inside by the time she reached her cabin.

As she fished her key card out of her purse, she turned back to find him still waiting.

Arms folded, one leg propped up against the post, he looked like something out of a dream.

She waved before ducking inside the door. Once it was closed, she leaned against it. Oh, she was in trouble.

It should be wrong to feel like this so soon after calling off things with Davis, but the heart wanted what it wanted.

And she wanted Caleb. Even if it was only for fun, until she had to return from this holiday vacation to the drudgery of real life, come January.

Chapter Ten

Sleep was hard to come by that night, so it was no surprise that Caleb was up well before sunrise. His alarm had been set for five a.m. to help for the morning fireside chats and ensure the breakfast service ran smoothly.

It was a quarter 'til five when he forced himself out of his room. His door closed too harshly, echoing in the long hall—the lights…ugh, far too bright for this early in the morning. The hair of the dog was all him, though. He hadn't gotten drunk in a very long time. Sure, he'd drunk his share of beers when he was in his depressed state. But never more than two in a sitting. Just enough to take the edge off.

He shielded his eyes as he walked under a fluorescent light. He needed coffee, stat.

He took the single flight of stairs down to the first floor. He badged out at the door leading from the staff quarters to the lobby. This early, it was eerily quiet. Evidence of last night's revelry wasn't hard to find.

Little bits of silver and red confetti scattered across the hardwood floor. A half-drunk bottle of beer nestled against the base of a potted plant. He picked up the bottle and started toward the kitchen. A tinkling jingle of bells drew his attention to the lobby. Where, of course, his mother stood behind the front desk, typing away at one of the computers.

The bells tinkled with every keystroke. "Mom," Caleb whispered. "What are you doing up?"

She looked up from the monitor, half-hidden in the massive oak front desk. "Drinking already?"

He let out a grunt. "Someone left this in a potted plant last night. I saw it on my way in." He pointed to the lipstick stain on the bottleneck. "Not exactly my shade, is it?"

Lainey reached across the desk to take it from him. "Hmm, it's warm, too. I'll take care of it. I was just tracking the shipment of Christmas presents to Emerson and Poppy. Olivia said they hadn't arrived yet, and I wanted to see what the hold-up was."

Caleb knew his ex-wife and mother talked. They'd never been each other's biggest fans when he was married to Olivia. Now that Olivia was no longer his wife, their focus was the kids, and they seemed to get along better.

"You made sure a couple of my gifts were in there, right? The small ones?"

"Of course. They'll open the rest at our house on New Year's Day. I'm not taking down any decorations until all my grandbabies have celebrated with us."

He frowned as a new wave of sadness overtook him. His mom didn't miss the shift in his expression.

"Oh, sweetheart. Christmas is more than just one day. We all miss them. But now it'll be extra special, right?"

His mother could be a royal pain in his ass, but there was no denying that she was the maker of Christmas magic, not just for the Ellises but for all Falling Leaves, as well.

"I know. I guess I've been trying not to think about it. Liv and Ashley deserve to have a Christmas with the kids without me butting in."

She came around the desk and laid a hand on his arm. "You're doing the right thing. We'll FaceTime them together this afternoon when you get back from your little excursion with Emma."

He groaned. Of course, the sweet moment couldn't last. "Mom, seriously. She's a guest. And I have kids — I can't just date anyone willy-nilly."

She rolled her eyes. "Who said anything about dating? My god, son. You dated one girl in high school. You married the one girl you dated in college. Maybe you should just have some fun before you look to settle down again. Who wants to go to their grave only having dated two people?"

"First of all, you're excluding Melody, my middle school girlfriend."

His mother took him by the elbow and led him away. "We don't count the girl you dated while you were still singing soprano in the church choir. Don't sidestep the point, Caleb. Emma is a nice girl."

"And, as activities director, I should keep my distance. I'm an employee, right?"

After pausing to set up the chairs around the fireplace for that morning's chat, they entered the dining room. It was still quiet at this hour, although he could hear the strains of Latin music coming from the kitchens.

"You're not even technically an employee of the lodge. Did you and your sister work out what your hourly rate would be?"

He stepped toward the closest table and began lowering chairs. "Now that you mention it, no. She said she was going to get back to me about it."

"I'll make sure to mention it to them when I see them later today. But to get back to my point." She set down a chair with a firm *thud* on the thick carpet. "This is a temporary job, with an end date. You work for Ellis & Daughter."

Caleb let out a soft grunt. Sometimes, he wondered if he should discuss renaming the business with his father.

However, he realized if he did that, he was committing to staying in Falling Leaves and taking over the business when his father retired. Something would have to change with the business. Ellis & Daughter wasn't so much a thing anymore. Sabrina's time was spent at Sky House. He wanted to take the business into a different direction. He'd tried numerous times to put his plans onto paper, but all he'd end up with were a few bullet points before he gave up.

He glanced up to find his mother pulling down chairs at the next table. "How come Sabrina didn't ask you to be the activities director? You're here half the time anyway."

Lainey's sweater jingled as she spun around. "First of all, my official title is 'Commander in Cheer', for which I am paid an annual salary, thank you very much."

She didn't say the quiet part out loud, for which Caleb was glad. He had this job because he'd worried his family. And whether he wanted to admit it, they'd been right to bring him here. He'd needed to crawl out of his depressive state.

"I'm going to go get a hangover cure from the kitchen while you keep pulling down chairs. I think we could both use it after last night, hmm?"

His mother made off for the kitchen as Caleb worked in silence. His mind automatically drifted to what he'd show Emma when they went into town. Of course, he was sure Sabrina probably had some scripted tour in mind, but seeing as neither of them would be here when they left, he could play it by ear.

Spending another day with Emma was worth looking forward to. As long as he remembered to keep his heart firmly in its place.

* * * *

Emma met Caleb at the lodge van at nine sharp. She'd had some tea and a piece of buttered toast, as that was all her stomach would tolerate. She hadn't drunk like that in years. Seeing Caleb gave her an altogether different sort of stomachache. That butterfly escaping its cage sort of feeling.

Caleb passed a to-go cup of coffee to her. "I hope you have an appetite. I have a treat in store for when we get to town."

"The longer I'm vertical, the better I feel." She nodded toward the van. "Is anyone else coming along? I just wanted to be sure if this was a casual thing or an employee/guest-sanctioned trip."

Caleb chuckled. "Technically, it's both. We offer tours into town a couple of times a week. Since it's Saturday, there are usually other people who come along. But we're not the only ones fighting off the hair of the dog this morning." He took a sip of his coffee and gazed at her over his cup. "That was a long way of saying it's just us. So, you can sit up front, or in the back if you want to feel fancy. It's just a van, either way."

She chuckled. "Front seat it is."

Caleb swung open the driver's-side door and leaned over as he placed his coffee cup in the center console. Emma tried hard not to notice how well his khakis fit his backside and broad thighs.

She failed.

He popped out of the car and walked around to open Emma's door for her. "My lady." He twirled with his left hand before offering it to help her into the van.

"You'd never know this was your first time offering this tour." She slipped into her seat.

"I've been here long enough to overhear the old activities director's speech before leading the tour. Because, of course, my sister has this tour timed down to the minute."

Caleb closed the door and ran around to the driver's side. Once he was buckled up, he turned to her. "I hope this doesn't make me look hopelessly uncool, but I need to wear glasses to drive."

She coughed to cover up the unintentional whimper that emanated. She was a total sucker for men in glasses. Instead of admitting this to Caleb and possibly freaking him out, she said, "Sure thing, Grandpa."

"We've already established that our age gap isn't glacial, thank you very much."

"Okay, okay. I'll just call you lodge man, then."

"Hey, now, that makes me sound like the guy on the side of a paper towel roll or something."

They came to the end of the long driveway. Caleb paused to look out for passing traffic before he pulled out onto the windy mountain road.

"I mean, I could see it? I'd ask you to cross your arms across your chest to be sure, but you're driving right now."

He chuckled. "The flannel uniform doesn't help things, that's for sure. Feel free to turn on the radio if you'd like."

The van had an old-fashioned radio, like the one Emma had in her first car. When she turned it on, she found only static.

"Oh yeah, we might not get reception until we get further down the mountain. If you want to risk it, I think there's a CD in there."

She pressed play. After the slight whirr of the CD spinning, a familiar song came over the speakers.

"Oh my god, *Dominick the Donkey*." Without thinking, she made a donkey noise before slapping a hand over her mouth. "Sorry. I used to love this song when I was a kid."

Caleb laughed. "This must be one of Brandon's CDs. I'm pretty sure I remember his parents playing this song at a Christmas party when we were teenagers."

"Wow, you've all known each other all that time?"

He shrugged. "Yes and no. Brandon and Sabrina were that usual story of a boy who loves a girl, the boy is a dick to said girl, then leaves for fancy Ivy League college when girl stays local. They reunited when they were renovating his family's inn in town."

"Of course, this town has an inn."

He laughed. "We nearly have two. The Westmores, who bought The Peculiar Pumpkin from Brandon, are opening a book-themed hotel next year. Although they're fighting with the town hall over whether it'll be an inn or a hotel. It's a whole thing."

"The inn is called The Peculiar Pumpkin. Book-themed hotel? Oh my god, this place sounds amazing."

"I don't want to oversell it or anything. It's still a small town in southwest Virginia with its own problems and a fair share of closed-minded dunderheads. God knows I ran from here as soon as I could. Now that I'm older, I can appreciate its charms."

She turned toward the window, admiring the snowy landscape. "Do you think you're back for good, then?"

The next song on the CD was Kelly Clarkson's *Underneath the Tree*. She hummed under her breath as Caleb inched the van over a patch of ice.

"Yeah, I think I'm back, if not for good, a while at least."

Emma had never been the small-town gal type. Originally from Prince George's County, Maryland, she'd spent most of her life in and around the DC metro area, aka the DMV. She'd always lived no more than a fifteen-minute drive from a metro station. She'd loved having the city at her fingertips. But now, she wasn't so sure. It would be rather depressing to get this chance for a big change, only to return to where she'd lived her whole life.

Only now she'd be on her own. Meaning, no more fancy Capitol Hill address. She'd probably have to get a roommate again.

Ugh.

She hated to admit that part of the reason she and Davis had stuck together was because they each got something out of the relationship other than romance. She kept his life ticking along—he never had to worry about mundane things like picking up dry cleaning, organizing cupboards, or arranging maintenance on the car.

She contributed to the expenses of his condo, but he'd never made her go fifty-fifty. Mainly because he'd had the condo when they met, and he had no interest in living anywhere where they could split things evenly.

She'd been spoiled, that was for sure.

"You okay?"

She tilted her head toward him, enjoying his side profile while his eyes stayed glued to the road.

"Yeah, I was just thinking about how big city life is so different from small towns."

He chuckled. "Believe me, I know that. I didn't apply to any colleges within one hundred and fifty miles of Falling Leaves. I ended up going to Duke. Durham isn't exactly a metropolis, but it's a hell of a lot bigger than Falling Leaves. What about you?"

Their conversation drifted back and forth, each revealing little bits about their lives as they wound down the mountain.

Roughly five miles out of town, they passed an elaborate wooden sign. *Falling Leaves, Five Miles Ahead* was written in a homey font against a background of Christmas trees and snowflakes.

"Given the town's name, autumn is our most popular tourist destination. But we're trying to increase our Christmas business with the lodge opening. They've added a lot of events. Since it's a Saturday, I suspect the town will be hopping."

As they drove into town, Emma craned her neck like a little kid on a ride, trying to take in everything.

Silver Spring Street was the main drag in town. Although it was barely ten a.m., nearly every parking spot was occupied. All the storefronts, including the hardware store, were decorated with Christmas cheer.

Each light post was decorated with garlands and fairy lights, and billowing flags welcomed visitors to town for a country Christmas.

This was something out of a storybook. How had an ad on social media led her to this perfect, life-changing place?

"You've gone quiet," Caleb observed.

She turned toward him, her gaze catching on grand Victorian manors as he rounded the corner. "It's…perfect, Caleb."

She half-expected him to make fun of her. Obviously, the magic had worn off for him, having grown up here. Instead, he reached over and gave her gloved hand a squeeze. Her heart raced at his touch.

"Wait until you meet the people. Then you may change your mind." They shared a smile.

Oh, shit. She was down bad not only for this town but for Caleb, as well.

Chapter Eleven

Caleb was thankful for the employees-only spot behind Loaved Up. He'd asked Sebastian to save it for them, knowing how difficult parking would be two Saturdays before Christmas.

As Emma chattered on about what she'd seen so far, he slipped his phone out of his pocket and texted his older brother.

We're here. And I swear to God, if you embarrass me, I will drive until I run out of gas and then bury your recipe box in the deepest hole I can find.

Of course, their mother had likely told Sebastian and his wife, Gretchen, about Emma. Embellishing, as she did. This was just a day trip around his hometown. A work trip, even.

His phone chimed with a new text.

As if I would do that. Come in when you're ready. I reserved the booth right by the window.

To anyone else, that text would seem almost kind. But Sebastian knew as well as anyone how this town worked. If his mother had told Sebastian about Emma, all the biddies knew as well. They would be on display for the whole town.

Thank god half the town was full of tourists today, making the microscope's glare a little easier to bear.

"You ready to go? My brother and sister-in-law are expecting us."

She was half out of the door before he finished his sentence. He chuckled as he followed suit. Before he could knock, the back door swung open. Thankfully, it was Gretchen, not Sebastian. She had better manners than his brother.

"Come on in! You arrived at the perfect time. We've had a bit of a lull now that the ice-skating rink opened."

"Ice skating?" Emma asked.

"A new addition to the winter festivities. Hi there, I'm Gretchen."

They stepped inside the bakery's back room. While Gretchen and Emma chitchatted, Caleb inhaled deeply. Loaved Up smelled like freshly brewed coffee and the bakery's famous yeasted cinnamon and chocolate rolls.

His brother had worked in big-city finance for years before pursuing his lifelong dream of opening a bakery. Caleb wished his dreams were as clear-cut as his siblings'. They'd always known what they wanted to do, even if it had taken them a while to achieve their goals.

After hanging up his coat, he pushed open the door to the bakery. He found Sebastian behind the counter, restocking the display case. He looked up as Caleb approached.

"Well? Where's your future Mrs.?"

"Shut the fu —"

He didn't get to finish that thought as Gretchen and Emma came behind Caleb. "Why don't you two get settled? We'll bring you over a sampler in a minute."

Sebastian stuck out his tongue. Suddenly, they were fourteen and twelve years old again, arguing over who was the better baseball player.

Emma's head pivoted back and forth like a marionette's.

Loaved Up was like a second home to Caleb. After all, he'd helped Sebastian and Gretchen gut and renovate the space before they'd opened for business late last year. The place was extra homey during the holidays. Christmas lights wound around the hearty wooden beams that crested across the ceiling, twinkling merrily. Tinsel and ornaments clung to anything that would sit still long enough, and the windows were painted with an old-fashioned winter scene.

The front booth was nestled into a bay window facing Silver Spring Street. From the window, they had a perfect view of the town gazebo and the ice-skating rink.

"Is it cold enough for ice to freeze today?" Emma asked.

"No. This is why the 'ice' is that glorified plastic stuff they put down in a lot of places now. It'll do in a pinch, though," Caleb said.

She scooted into the booth. "I used to love to ice skate when I got the chance. I haven't in ages, though."

Caleb slipped into the booth opposite her. "Well, it's your day in town. If you want to ice skate, I'm sure we can make it happen for you."

She gestured to the line snaking around the outside of the gazebo. "Maybe today isn't the best day for that. I don't have to do everything today. I'm staying at the lodge until after Christmas."

Her smile drooped, but Gretchen appeared with a three-tiered metal and wood tray before he had time to ask if anything was bothering her.

"This is the holiday sampler."

While Gretchen went through the items on each level of the tray, Caleb couldn't keep his eyes off Emma. Her dark hair cascaded over one side of her face as she leaned forward. Her lips were painted a shade of red that suited her pale coloring.

What was going on with him? He was never the type of guy to notice the little details. It was one of the things he and Olivia had argued about. One of the biggest fights they had was when it'd taken him two days to notice that she'd gotten over four inches cut off her hair.

He knew well enough that it was probably a symptom of a deeper issue with his relationship with Olivia. But still, he wasn't the type to be wooed by lipstick.

"Where should we start, Caleb?"

"I'll go get a coffee flight sampler while you two figure it out," Gretchen said.

Caleb pointed to the bottom row of the tray, where slabs of several of Sebastian's most popular breads lay, along with various spreads.

"Try the signature loaf first. It's the thing that gets butts in seats, as my brother says."

He handed Emma a plate, his fingers brushing hers as she took it. Her cheeks flushed the same pinkish red as her dress.

Jesus Christ.

She ducked her cheek against her shoulder as she reached for a piece. "Sounds like a plan."

"Don't forget the butter and jam." He nodded toward the small container on the table.

Gretchen returned with the coffee flight—several small cups of their locally sourced brews.

After she left them again, Caleb looked around for Sebastian. Thankfully, his older brother was nowhere to be found. They had the space to themselves, however momentarily.

"You look like you're having fun," he observed.

She wiggled slightly in her seat. "I am! It's kind of invigorating and depressing at the same time. I realized that I haven't felt like this in ages."

"Why depressing?"

She was thoughtful while she buttered her bread. "I guess I was feeling a kind of anticipatory grief for a while. Do you know what that is?"

Caleb shook his head.

"I think I knew my old life was dying. So, when I lost my job, I lost Davis, and I wasn't as devastated as I should've been. Because, in a way, I'd been grieving that life for a while now."

He draped his arm along the back of the booth. "Have you heard from him at all since he left?"

She rolled her eyes slightly. "Just a message that I had until the end of January to get my stuff out of his condo. I don't know. I'm not mad at him. Just a little relieved, I guess."

"That's a very mature way of looking at it, Emma."

She shrugged. "What can I say, I've had a lot of time to think about it." She took a bite of bread. "So, what will we do next if ice skating is out? Maybe a little window shopping? Or actual shopping?"

He grinned. "Oh, I have an itinerary planned, don't you worry. It's been a while since I've been able to show off my hometown to anyone, and I intend to take good advantage of it."

She laughed. "By all means, take all the advantage you want." She seemed to notice the innuendo only after the words were out of her mouth. "Within reason, of course."

He covered his smile with a napkin. "But of course."

* * * *

After they left Loaved Up, Caleb suggested that they walk through downtown. She'd noticed that there was only one stoplight through the center of town, so she readily agreed.

Snow began to lightly fall as they descended Silver Spring Street. "Is it a requirement that every business name be a pun?" She nodded to the hardware store, Missing Screw.

Caleb chuckled. "It's actually in the town charter, yes." He turned to find her staring at him incredulously. "I'm kidding, sorry. This place just loves puns. My uncle and cousin own the hardware store." He pointed ahead to The Weird Sisters, the town's metaphysical shop. "That's not a pun."

"It is a Shakespeare reference," she retorted. She half-listened to his reply, her eyes drawn to the empty shop two over from The Weird Sisters.

"That's the Ellis & Daughter headquarters there." Caleb pointed next door. "No puns there."

"It's a cute little space," Emma said.

"Just a small showroom with supplies and a place to meet clients. Our previous office was over in The Missing Screw. My cousin Dennis took over the business earlier this year and wanted it as his office. The whole thing was Sabrina's idea, but then she jumped ship to work at Sky House."

Emma's gaze stayed focused on the empty shopfront. "Does she still work with the business?"

"Yes, usually more in the summer. We now have an assistant who helps run the business. I've taken over as a contractor, so we do okay." He stepped closer to Emma. "It really is a cute little space, huh?"

A striped awning jutted out above the door. Writing that had faded too much to read had been scraped off the front door. It was painted slate gray, but scraps of a sunny yellow paint showed through where it was peeling. She cupped her hands to her face and peered in.

The shop was a shotgun space—straight up and down. She could see through the entire space. Shelves haphazardly lined the walls. At the rear of the store was an old-fashioned wooden table, likely serving as the cash rep.

"Whatcha looking at?" Caleb said. "Has another raccoon gotten loose?"

Her breath obscured the view into the shop. "This is the shop you were talking about, isn't it? Y'know, for my hypothetical stationery store."

"It's small but could work in your case."

A breeze blew down the street. Without thinking, she took a step toward him. His large body shielded her from the wind.

"Maybe it's a silly dream, but it's always been stored up in the back of my mind. It was always out of reach in the city. There are a lot of high-end stationery stores in DC."

And New York, which was why Davis' half-hearted promise to help her find space was nothing more than a trick to get her to go along with him. Even though Davis did very well for himself, opening a business like that in New York would've been out of reach without hefty investment.

But here...she wasn't sure. She'd be the first to admit she was the type to hoard her money. Her chaotic upbringing had shown her that anything could change in a heartbeat. Being prepared helped stave off heartbreak.

Her savings were in decent shape. More than decent, she supposed. She invested and didn't spend fruitlessly.

Caleb's voice cut into her thoughts. "Well, this used to be the town's running and outdoor shop. They moved to a bigger space around the corner. It's been empty for a few months now."

A shiver of excitement lit her up from head to toe. "It's silly," she said. "I've only been here for an hour, but it feels like someplace I could stay. Is that weird?" She gazed up to find his eyes already meeting hers. A secondary shiver rippled through her body.

"This is the kind of place you can fall in love with. I'm proud to call it my home."

Another gust of wind blew down the street, sending Caleb's hat flying away.

"Shit!"

He took off at a run, with Emma following. They both laughed as they ran, careful to avoid tourists casually strolling. He caught up to his hat in the middle of Silver Spring Street, where it had landed in a puddle.

He groaned as it dripped onto his hand. "Do you mind if we stop at my place so I can get another hat? It's too cold out here to be without one."

She blushed at what was likely a harmless invitation. But it'd been a very long time since any man had invited her back to his place, so her brain once again leaped out in front of her.

"It's just around the corner. We can head to Broadmere Books after."

She fell into step next to him. "Sure."

"And just for your information, I have it on good authority that no one has shown a peep of interest in that space since the other shop left. But it is the only open space of that size in town. Making it a prime location."

She laughed. "Way to indulge my delusions, Caleb."

"You say delusions. I say dreams." He flashed her another grin as he fished his keys out of his jeans pocket.

Oh, she was in a world full of trouble.

Chapter Twelve

Caleb fiddled with the lock. The old thing was finnicky on a good day. The door creaked open, and he got a whiff of a familiar Christmassy scent. The room spray used at the lodge. He ducked his head in and found his apartment had been tidied by either Sabrina or his mother. Normally, he hated their interference, but just this once, he was glad for it.

He turned to Emma, finding a distant look in her eyes. He cleared his throat. "Um, I just realized that inviting you to my apartment might've come off weird. I hope I didn't overstep. I really do just want my hat."

Emma's eyes snapped to focus. "Sorry? I was thinking about that shop. I don't think it's weird that you invited me up here."

He cleared his throat. Well, maybe this feeling was one-sided, then. He could've sworn there was something between the two of them. Instead of dwelling on that, he pushed open the door.

"It'll take me just a second to grab a hat. Provided my mom didn't rearrange things the last time she was here."

Emma stepped inside and looked around.

Late morning sunlight streamed in through the parted curtains. The left-hand side of the room was a brick wall, with windows stacked on top of each other. The drafts could be a real bitch this time of year.

The building was old, but his apartment had been redone by Ellis & Daughter as a rental property some years back. The style was all Sabrina's. Slick subway tile in the kitchen, wooden butcher-block counters. She'd refinished the old floors. They looked nice, but still creaked every time he moved.

"Wow. This is such a nice space for a bachelor pad."

He snorted as the front door swung shut on its own. Another lovely feature of living in a hundred-and-forty-year-old building.

"My kids live here every other weekend, so it's not quite the bachelor pad you think. As you can see, there's no closet, so all my things are in my room. I'll be right back." He headed down the hall.

"Don't worry, I'll have a nose around while you're not watching," she called after him.

He chuckled to himself. She was something else.

He rushed past his daughters' half-open bedroom door. Peeking in, it was confirmed that it was his mother who'd been there. She'd left gifts on each of the girls' beds. His mother and the other biddies fundraised every Christmas to wrap presents for town folks, so there was no missing her signature style, complete with ribbons and string galore. And the tags were signed with love from Mimi and Gramps.

He left the room before he could get too emotional about missing his kids. Funny how, since he'd started working at the lodge, the wound ached a little less.

Emma's presence didn't hurt, either. He half-wondered if she felt the same. Were they both working on healing a heartache?

He grabbed a hat out of his top drawer and walked back to the living room. There, he found Emma half-bent over, looking at photos atop the old wooden mantle. The fireplace hadn't worked since the Reagan administration, but the old mantle did look nice, especially with his mother's handmade stockings hanging with care.

Emma turned when he approached. "If I didn't know better, I'd swear a woman lived here." She spoke with a teasing tone, no malice.

"That woman is my mother. She gave my place a clean. She's kind of a pain in the ass, but what are you going to do? She's not the toxic, overbearing type, if you were worried. She respects my boundaries most of the time." He realized what he'd said and began to stutter. "Uh, why would you be worried? Sorry, that was weird. Again. I've got to stop doing that."

Emma rose to standing. "It's not weird." She arched an eyebrow before reaching for a photo of his girls. "Which one's which?"

It took him a second to process that request as his brain whirled around like he'd just gotten off a carnival ride. Was she flirting with him?

He cleared his throat. "The older one is Emerson. She's five. Poppy is two and a half."

She touched the corner of the frame. "They're freaking adorable."

He tugged on his hat. "This is the longest I'll ever have gone without seeing them. But my ex and I are a pretty good team. There are rough patches, of course. But that's parenting."

Emma set the frame back on the mantle. "So, where are we going next?"

He took a half-step toward her. "I was thinking we could stop by The Peculiar Pumpkin. Brandon used to own it before he and Sabrina opened the lodge."

She bumped against his chest. "Oof, I'm sorry. I didn't realize—"

Without thinking, his hand came to her cheek, still rosy from the cold.

Her beauty overtook him. She gazed up at him, her eyes bright, mouth parted. He rubbed his thumb against her cheek.

"Emma, if you don't mind, I'd really like to kiss you."

Once, Emma had wondered if she'd ever feel butterflies again. She'd assumed that they died off the longer you were with someone. It was natural, given the complexities of daily living.

But the way Caleb looked at her—there was no business there. All butterflies.

She realized she'd been staring at him without saying a word. It was his fault for having the kind of hazel eyes you could get lost in.

He cleared his throat and started to step away. "I'm sorry. I meant it when I said I invited you up here with no ill intention. I guess I…"

He trailed off as Emma brought her index finger to his lips. "I mean this in the nicest way possible, but you don't strike me as the type to be underhanded, Caleb.

If you wanted to kiss me, you would've done it in the van, on the street corner…or here."

He reached for her hand and cradled it against his. "You're right about that."

Their eyes locked in another moment before Caleb leaned down, taking her face in his hands.

"Last chance to back out."

Their eyes met. She exhaled and brought her hands to the front of his coat, pulling him closer as the kiss quickly deepened. Caleb kept one hand on her face, and the other looped around her waist, leaving no space between them.

Her feet came off the ground as she wrapped her arms around his neck.

It was as if time slowed down. She wasn't sure how long they'd been kissing when he pulled away, leaving her gasping for air. "Why did you stop?"

He dropped her back to the ground before taking a step back. "I…don't know what got into me."

Emma rubbed at her newly bruised lips. "I think we both know what got into you. Please don't overthink this, Caleb. That kiss was enough to build a dream on, but it doesn't have to be anything if you don't want it to be. I'm just here for the holiday, probably, maybe, remember?"

The words were half true to her. But he didn't need to know that. The last thing she wanted to do was freak him out by saying Falling Leaves felt like home.

Especially if he was merely interested in a holiday fling. Caleb was a proper grown-up, complete with kids! She wasn't sure she was ready for what came with that sort of relationship.

As if he could read her mind, he said, "I'm not the casual type, Emma. I've had three girlfriends in my entire life, going back to middle school. Sure, I've dated casually here and there—mostly setups by my friends and family. But I don't do things halfway. I don't want there to be a problem between us."

He was so thoughtful that it bordered on being sweet and *almost* annoying. This was not a man who would break her heart on purpose, which made her want him even more.

She stepped closer to him. "I would like for you to kiss me again, Caleb. But I understand if you'd rather not right now. Did you want to go to the Pumpkin place? The inn? That sounds fun." She rested her hand on the crook of his arm. She could sense the muscle there even under several layers of winter clothing.

He slipped his hat over his dark hair. "I think that would be fun. But I'd also understand if—"

"*Caleb.* You did nothing wrong. I've known you for three days, and that's long enough to know you're an honorable man. I like spending time with you." She stood on her tiptoes and gave him a quick kiss on the lips.

"See? That time, it was me. Now come on, I'm dying to see what a Halloween-themed inn looks like all decorated for Christmas."

She turned for the door, Caleb's soft laugh echoing behind her. "Whatever you say, Emma."

By the time they stepped back onto a frigid Silver Spring Street, any awkwardness had passed. She tugged her gloves back on as Caleb took her hand, leading her to the crosswalk.

"I don't know why they have this—nearly everyone in town jaywalks." He nodded to a group of tourists, giggling as they ran across to the other side of the street.

"Well, if you've got one stoplight, it makes sense that there would be a crosswalk to go with it," Emma said.

She allowed him to lead her across the street. The Peculiar Pumpkin was catty-cornered to them. The grand old Victorian house stood apart from the others in town, with its black paint and violet shutters.

Caleb pointed to the house. "The Peculiar Pumpkin is an institution in this town. It was one of the first tourist attractions, back when this was just a place you stopped to get gas on the way to Roanoke."

"Was it like that when you were a kid? Or was it already charming?"

They stopped before the B&B, sidestepping a group of elderly tourists.

"Eh, it was rustically charming, I guess. Many of the houses were in disrepair. That'll happen when a lot of them are more than a hundred years old. The town didn't get this charming until about ten years ago, when Mayor Ford was elected. He's really helped turn the place around."

They stepped onto the covered porch. Emma took in the black Christmas tree, which was adorned with red, black and green ornaments.

"They stay on theme at the Pumpkin," Caleb said.

No sooner had he finished speaking than one of the double doors to the inn swung open. A stunning redhead stepped out, a toddler on her hip.

"Caleb Ellis, I heard a rumor that you may be making your way over here." Her accent was as thick as honey.

"Given that gossip spreads like butter in this town, I'm not surprised," Caleb deadpanned. He turned to Emma. "This is Merit Westmore. She and her husband run several hotels around the world, but the Pumpkin is their home base."

The little girl reached across her mother for Caleb. "Ca-Ca," she said.

Emma snorted as Caleb laughed. "It's an unfortunate nickname. But little Lakyn seems to like me."

Merit passed her daughter over to Caleb, who, of course, was a natural. "I think Lakyn knows he's a girl dad, huh, baby girl?"

Emma watched as Caleb bobbed the little girl in his arms.

Caleb already had children. Since she'd never wanted any kids of her own, it'd always been a somewhat tricky subject to navigate. Because to share her reasoning meant having to delve into her own childhood trauma. Not that she was getting ahead of herself or anything. They'd simply kissed.

Merit's voice cut into her thoughts. "You have any kids of your own, Emma?"

She shook her head. She'd learned to avoid the subject until she got to know someone well. Which meant she should tell Caleb at some point. If he wanted this thing between them to be more than a kiss.

Caleb handed the little girl back to her mother, his eyes carefully on Emma. "How about we go inside and get something to warm up? The Frosted Squash has a fantastic lunch special today."

"That sounds wonderful."

Merit walked ahead of them through the door. Caleb held it open for them with one hand, and with his other, he reached for Emma's.

She looked up at him, finding comfort in his touch and his soft expression. Of all the extraordinary things that had occurred in the last seventy-two hours, she wondered if this feeling would lose its shine the longer she was around him.

But as he pulled her closer as they stepped into the lobby, Emma decided that, for now, she was done worrying about what might be.

Fate had brought her to this place and literally into the path of this man.

"You okay, Emma? You looked a little far away back there."

Emma gazed up at the chandelier in the lobby. The little crystal droplets threw light around the cozy space.

"Oh, don't you worry about me. I was just…thinking. About things." She grinned at him. It wasn't exactly a lie. Her brain had replayed a slow-mo of their kiss between her worries.

"Yes, things." He slipped a hand onto her hip.

Butterflies took flight once more.

Chapter Thirteen

"Are you sure you want to skip skating?" Caleb gestured to where a smattering of folks lined up.

"That's because it's colder than frozen moose shit out here," Emma said.

Caleb snorted. "That's an expression I can't say I've heard before."

"I got it from Pa Henderson. Besides, this isn't the only time I have to see the town, right?"

Caleb cut a glance at Emma. He'd had a fabulous day with her, and the thought of having another made him feel a little giddy. Funny how he'd gone without that kind of feeling so long, he'd almost forgotten how it'd felt.

"You're right. Better to get back to the lodge before dark, anyhow." He placed a hand on her back, leading her toward Loaved Up.

"We should make it back in time for dinner," Emma said. "Do you have any activities you have to run tonight, or do you think we could...?"

He met her gaze. "We can have dinner. There's only bingo tonight, and Babs and Inez run that. Although they're hustlers, I wouldn't be surprised if they found a way to cheat at bingo."

She smiled and turned away from him. "How would they do that? Rig the balls so they come out in a certain order?"

"I'm kind of glad they're content with running Falling Leaves and haven't turned their attention to the international crime syndicate."

Emma laughed. "Well, I'm glad you're free. Let me pull up the menu for tonight before we lose cell coverage."

Between his mother, Sabrina and Brandon, the lodge seemed to run just fine on its own. No wonder the last person who had this job brought her boyfriend up to the mountain to pass the time.

He knew better than to ask Sabrina about it. He loved his family, but they weren't above lying for the greater good, as they called it. Besides, he'd probably get tricked into admitting that Sabrina had been right about luring him out of his apartment. He wasn't quite ready to face her gloating just yet.

Because she would—he wouldn't have met Emma had he stayed up in his apartment for the remainder of December. He couldn't deny that there was something spectacular about the woman walking beside him. He just wished he could let go and allow himself to enjoy living in the moment. Why did he have to be a monogamous weirdo? Why did every relationship have the end goal of commitment?

They rounded the corner to the parking lot behind Loaved Up. Emma held up her phone.

"The chicken pot pie sounds good. Have you had it?"

"Nearly everything at the lodge is amazing. Brandon poached the chef from a fancy hotel in DC, where he used to work."

"Oh yeah? Which one?"

"Hotel Blaque," Caleb said.

She laughed. "I've been to that restaurant before! I used to live not too far from there. Small world, huh?"

He grinned. "I guess it is."

The car ride passed in what felt like moments. Rather than risking a non-stop loop of *Dominick the Donkey,* they chatted companionably about nothing in particular. When he pulled the van into the circular drive in front of the lodge, he turned off the engine.

"How about if we reconvene at seven-thirty? I need to check in a few places before dinner."

Emma nodded. "Of course. You're still on the clock." She reached for the door handle.

He wanted to be a gentleman, so he quickly bolted out of the van and ran around to her side.

When the door opened, Emma was laughing. "You ran around the front of the van like your ass was on fire."

He leaned in the doorframe. "Can't have a lady getting out of the van on her own. What kind of man would I be?"

He extended his gloved hand. She held onto it for a moment. "I had a really great day today, Caleb. I want to go back to Falling Leaves again soon."

He grinned. "I can make that happen. Any day but tomorrow, as that's the sledding competition."

She laughed. "Fair enough. That sounds like too good of a spectacle to miss, anyhow."

He helped her down, and she finally released his hand. "I'll see you in a little bit."

Caleb took the long back way into the lodge. He wanted to avoid his sister and the biddies, who were likely setting up for bingo. He wasn't sure he could keep the loopy look off his face. He wasn't in the mood to answer questions.

On his way to his room, his phone chimed with a video call. He smiled when he saw it was from Olivia. As soon as he accepted the call, his daughters' faces popped up on the screen.

"Daddy!" The wind half-carried their voices away, as it looked like they were at a ski resort.

"How are you, Daddy? We miss you," Emerson said.

His heart welled in his throat. He'd gotten used to missing his girls. Olivia and Ashley had primary custody. It made sense—they had a big house with a backyard and a dog. He'd been stuck in his apartment since the divorce.

"Hi, girls, whatcha doing?" He badged in through one of the doors marked "Employees Only."

"Skiing! Just me, though, Poppy's still a baby."

"Am not!" Poppy began to whine.

Okay, maybe he didn't miss the way his girls picked at each other. Emerson had Olivia's big, bold personality, while Poppy was quieter, like him. Sometimes, parenting felt more like refereeing. Perhaps it was his penance for the constant infighting he and his siblings put their parents through throughout their childhood.

Olivia appeared behind the girls. "Ashley's still on the slopes, so we're having a little après-ski break until she gets back." She set two cups of hot cocoa in front of the girls, who quickly began fishing out marshmallows. And bickering. He smiled. Even when they were going at it, his kids were adorable.

"How are you, Caleb? You look good."

He wanted to tell Olivia about his day, but he hesitated. This thing with Emma felt like something *huge*. But that anxious voice in his head told him to take things slow.

Besides, he had the girls to worry about. He wouldn't introduce anyone to them unless things were serious.

"Good. Busy, but that's a good thing. Staying in the holiday spirit."

Olivia cocked an eyebrow. *"Really?* Is there a particular reason — or a person — you're feeling so holly jolly?"

Thankfully, he was saved from having to answer by the girls.

"We get a second Christmas when we get home. Did you know that?" Poppy interjected.

The girls started to chatter on again as Caleb arrived in his room. He stayed on the call until it was time for them to return to the slopes.

* * * *

"Wait a minute, slow down," Aniyah said. "You kissed this guy? Less than seventy-two hours after handing Davis back his ring?"

Emma bit her lip. *Shit, maybe it was a bit of a rush.*

Aniyah noticed her expression and chuckled. "That was *not* judgment I was passing, Em. I'm impressed." She held up her hand to her phone, wanting an air high-five.

Emma began to fret. "No, you're right. I'm a terrible person. I forced my fiancé to come on this trip with me. I gave him the ring back, and I'm already hooking up with someone else."

Aniyah leaned back on her bed, adjusting her pillows as she fell back. "First of all, a kiss is not a hook-up. Secondly, you are the farthest from a terrible person I know, Em. You deserve happiness. I hope you can remember what it feels like after so long."

Aniyah had never been shy about her views on Davis. But she'd long told Emma that he didn't have to make her happy — only Emma. And if Emma was happy, that was all that mattered. Emma, of course, had lied and said she was. Because Aniyah would've shown up with her husband and a moving truck otherwise.

"You thought I was happy with Davis all that time."

She snorted. "No, I didn't. Look, I would've gotten you out of there if he was anything other than a self-absorbed asshole."

"Straight up the middle of the road," Emma and Aniyah said together. It'd been one of Pa Henderson's favorite sayings.

Aniyah laughed. "Exactly. This guy isn't, though."

Caleb was the furthest thing from it. "He makes me feel like Times Square on New Year's Eve," Emma said.

"Okay, I'm going to take the metaphor as you laid it out, but right now, I'm thinking about how those people wait all day and use diapers so they don't lose their spots."

Emma snorted. "Okay, lose the metaphor. Today felt like it went by in a second, yet it was, alternatively, three weeks long. I feel like a different person now than when I left this morning."

"This is all good stuff, Em! So why do I get a feeling there's a big old but coming?"

She covered her face with her free hand. "Because I'm at a major crossroads! I have no job, no place to live. Caleb has kids — he needs someone stable, you know?"

"Wait, he has kids? Seriously?"

Emma lowered her hand, taking in her sister. "Yeah. Which makes it weird."

Does it? It'd been so long since she'd dated anyone new, she wasn't sure. Davis had been upfront from the start — it was one of the things that had made her fall for him so quickly. Some men didn't even know they wanted kids until they realized *she* didn't want any. They'd start prying, and she'd end up trauma dumping all over some guy. Many men sought a 'normal' partner. And kids usually came along with that.

"Only if you allow it to be. And look, we're talking long-term, anyway. You said the ex is out of town with the kids until the holidays are over. So, if this is just a fling, the kids will never come into play."

"And if it's not?"

"Then you'll all deal with it, like grown-ups. But please, don't put the brakes on this already, Em. I know you feel bad since you and Davis just ended things. But we both know that relationship has been on life support since before he put a ring on it."

Why was her heart suddenly in her throat? She stared at her best friend's face and exhaled. Aniyah was right. She'd always had a terrible habit of living two steps ahead instead of enjoying the moment.

"I know. I'm going to try to slow my roll and live in the moment."

Aniyah chuckled. "You've never been very good at that. But hey, now is a perfect time to reinvent yourself.

I'd start with being forthright with Caleb about what this thing between you is. I think that will take a lot of stress off the both of you."

"Define it, even if that definition is holiday fling?"

"Exactly. Get over that awkward hump before you can do some actual humping."

Emma groaned. "Goodbye, Aniyah. I'll talk to you tomorrow."

"Don't overthink it!" Aniyah called before Emma ended the call.

If only it were that simple to shut off her brain.

A sharp knock on the door brought her back to reality. She'd asked the front desk for more towels so she could shower before meeting Caleb. She tossed her phone face down on the bed and crossed the short distance to the door. Her eyes caught on the Christmas lights wrapped around the tree in the corner.

She'd miss this place when it was time to leave. Somehow, it felt like home already.

She swung open the door and found Caleb.

"Are you up for room service?"

Chapter Fourteen

Emma eyed the boxes cradled against Caleb's forearm. Of course, he'd changed and freshened up before coming over. Brand new flannel. And his smell…it was like the woodsy aroma found in the lodge's main building, but there was something else, too.

If it was his natural scent, she was hooked.

"Emma?"

She blinked to consciousness. Caleb's expression had shifted. His eyes were full of worry.

"Sorry, I got…distracted. Come in."

She stepped aside and let him into her cabin. "I realized on the way over here I should've called to be sure it was okay. But then my arms were full, I couldn't remember the number to this cabin, and then I realized I don't even have your phone number…" Emma took the containers from him.

"You're fine, Caleb! I was going to take a shower, but unless I'm nose blind, I don't think I smell too bad."

He cleared his throat. "You smell just fine. I think. I mean, I'm not close enough, really..." She had to wonder if he was thinking the same thing she was...

You can come closer if you want to.

She swallowed down a cheeky reply. She didn't want to weird him out, especially after their earlier kiss. He was tentative, and she didn't want to take advantage of that. "Good to know. Let's eat, huh?"

They set up at the small kitchenette. Caleb had thought of everything, even bringing them both a couple of beers. And water. And soda.

He was so thoughtful she worried her heart might explode.

They settled into the small kitchen table. The space was so tight their knees touched.

"I should prepare you for bingo," he said. "The biddies run their bingo games like they belong in a Vegas gambling hall. Which, on occasion, includes musical acts and scantily dressed waiters."

Emma chuckled. "High rollers only? Do I need to stop at the ATM before we head over there?"

"C-notes only," Caleb joked as he took the lids off their food.

"Ooh, that pot pie looks divine." Emma reached her fork toward the container. "Thank you for remembering. You're very thoughtful."

"I try to be," he said simply.

They fell into silence while they set out their food. She took her first bite and let out a low, pleased sound.

"Yum."

She caught Caleb's quirked eyebrow and nearly choked. "I'm sorry. My love affair with carbs is lifelong."

He snapped open his beer can. "Same. I'll toast to that."

She opened her beer and clinked her can against his. "I had a really good time with you today, Caleb. I'm kind of glad the day isn't quite over."

He scratched at his beard. "Me too. I was worried you'd be sick of me after all day together in town."

"I had the best day in like…a long time. December can be a tricky month for me."

He cleared his throat. "Are the holidays hard for you, usually?"

Emma stabbed at a gooey blob of chicken and vegetables. "Yes, and no. I learned to set my expectations low. I'd usually visit Davis' family wherever they were spending the holiday that year. It was rarely in Ottawa, where he's from. They're very upper-class. The type to discuss mathematical theorems and world politics over dinner. A bit much for a former foster kid."

He cleared his throat. "I'm sure you've seen by now that my family is kind of a wild bunch. I wouldn't have it any different, though. Even if sometimes I have to go sit in a dark room and breathe for a few minutes. They can be overstimulating."

Emma smiled. "I get that. Life at the Hendersons was kind of nuts. There were us foster kids and the Hendersons had their kids and grandkids. I kind of miss it. Even though Aniyah—my foster sister—and I would sometimes 'go for a walk' to get away from the chaos." She mimed holding a cigarette to her mouth.

Caleb laughed. "Oh, so we're the same that way then. Mom would always fuss about how when my cousins and I would come back from one of our walks, we smelled like the devil's lettuce."

She brought her hand to her mouth to keep food from flying out. "I should've expected that from you. Wild middle child."

He nudged her slightly with his elbow. "And to top it off, I've always been one more for natural remedies, if you catch my drift. My sister always says I smell like patchouli and nag champa. It's just the soap I use."

"You'll have to tell me what soap it is."

Their eyes met. He reached over to squeeze her hand. "These last couple of days have shaken me out of my winter blues."

"And you've helped take my mind off of..." She pointed to her bare ring finger. She worried that she felt *too* happy only days out of a long-term relationship. Clearly, she'd made the right choice.

His face softened. "I guess we've been good for each other, huh?"

She leaned forward, bringing their mouths together. "Yes, I think we are."

* * * *

"High stakes bingo! Come get your pull tabs here!" Babs stood by the front door, her wacky Christmas sweater haphazardly blinking red and green Christmas lights.

"I don't know if my sister and brother-in-law would want you to be running a gambling ring out of the lodge."

Babs lowered her glasses to the tip of her nose and rolled her eyes at him. "Of course, everything is legal. See, Eleanor is over there!" She pointed inside the lounge. "Would we really be running an illegal gambling ring if the recently retired sheriff of Falling Leaves was in attendance?"

"I suppose not," Caleb said carefully.

"So, if you want to come, you'll need to pony up the dough. The minimum is twenty dollars, six dollars per sheet. Pull tabs start at three dollars and increase from there. We'll have a special raffle mid-tournament. The prize is a room refresh renovation from Ellis & Daughter!"

Caleb snorted. "That's news to me. But hardly the first time my sister has signed me up for something without telling me first."

Emma reached for her wallet before Caleb got the chance. "You got dinner, I'll get the…gambling."

Caleb was desperate to get away from Babs, whose gaze was currently darting back and forth between them like she was watching a tennis match.

Once she'd bought several pull tabs and bingo sheets, they made their way into the lounge. Nearly every table was full, save for one in the back, next to his parents.

"Caleb, are you okay?" Emma's hand came to his arm.

He leaned down to speak to her over the noise. "The only table left is next to my parents. You sure you haven't had enough of my family?"

She laughed as she angled herself against him. "Davis' parents used to quiz me on Canadian politics. They had a buzzer when I got the answer wrong. I'm not even Canadian! Yours can't be as bad."

"Well, I guess we have no choice but to find out, as my mom just spotted us."

Lainey Ellis stood and began waving her arms. "Caleb! Emma! Over here!"

Emma gave his arm a squeeze. "We can handle it. And if not, booze will help."

He exhaled. Even amidst the chaos of nearly a hundred guests and Falling Leaves locals piling in for bingo, Emma gave off a calming air.

He just hoped that it wouldn't disappear the longer she sat next to his mother.

Lainey came around the table and ambushed them. "I was hoping you two would show up tonight! Emma, have you met Caleb's dad Glen yet?"

His dad, to his credit, gave a half-hearted wave before turning back to watching a basketball game on his phone. Dad knew as well as he did that his mom would give him a hard time if she found him on his phone once bingo started.

Emma and Lainey began chatting amicably. Perhaps he was harder on his mom than he should be. Even though he'd been back in town for over a year, he still wasn't quite used to her being a part of his day-to-day life.

His dad looked up as he sat down. "I ordered you two a couple of beers — they should be here shortly. I figured you'd need them."

Caleb chuckled. "Hey, while I've got a minute with you, I was wondering if we could get a meeting on the books for early next year. To discuss the future of the business and all that."

Glen turned his phone face down on the table. "Did you get another job, Caleb? If you did, don't worry about me. We can figure it out."

His father wouldn't ask for help if he were dangling off a cliffside. He was the stoic type, no matter what. Last year, Sabrina and their mother had almost lost their minds trying to get him to attend his therapy sessions after surgery.

"I haven't applied for a teaching job in months, Dad. Not that environmental engineering jobs are *that* plentiful in this part of Virginia anyhow."

"Then what is it?"

Caleb shot a glance behind him to be sure Emma wasn't in over her head with Lainey. The two chatted as if they'd known each other forever.

"I was thinking maybe it's time for me to take a bigger stake in the business. I know Sabrina is working with the inn more during the busy winter season. Come spring, she'll have more time to work on jobs. But we could expand the business beyond what it is now."

Glen smiled. "Haven't seen that spark in your eyes for a while, son. What were you thinking?"

Since so much of their business revolved around renovating older homes, he was always looking for ways to make the builds more environmentally friendly. He'd come up with a half-hearted business proposal to add environmental services to the business — consulting, sales, that sort of thing.

It wasn't fully fleshed out yet, but he thought there was real promise in the business.

Feedback screeched through the room as Babs approached the microphone. Caleb brought his hands to his ears.

"Sorry, sorry. It's time to get started now, everybody. Please take your seats."

"Can we talk about it after the holidays? I want to get all my thoughts together."

Glen chuckled. "Sure. I'm looking forward to it."

* * * *

"Okay, hustler." Caleb bumped his elbow against Emma's.

She fanned herself with a stack of twenty-dollar bills. She'd not only won bingo twice but had also won third prize in the nightly raffle — a dinner date for two to Luci's, the finest restaurant in town.

"Should I have mentioned that I used to play bingo with the Hendersons once a week in the church basement? And it was how Ma Henderson funded her twice-yearly Caribbean cruises? Maybe I should've mentioned that."

He pointed to the corner where the biddies were eyeing her with a mix of awe and frustration.

"Well, I'm not saying you had to, but I'm not so sure they'll be inviting you back for next month's bingo."

As soon as the words passed his lips, he regretted them. Emma wouldn't be here next month. She'd be back to her big city life.

Wouldn't she?

Emma waved to the biddies with her free hand as they left the lounge. "I'll have to remember that," was all she said.

Not exactly a confirmation or a denial of her future plans. He took a breath. Maybe it was time to pump the brakes on this. It'd only been a handful of days, yet he felt like Emma had been in his life forever.

The lounge was still bustling with activity, but the rest of the lodge was settled down for the night. Only a few guests were huddled around the large fireplace, talking.

Funny how he'd balked when Brandon and Sabrina had shown them this place. But after they'd shared their vision, he'd been on board. Now, they were living the dream.

"You okay?" Emma asked.

He exhaled. "Yeah. Just a little tired."

She yawned into the crook of her arm. "It's been a long day. A good one, though."

"Yeah, a good one." He held open the back door leading to the cabins. A burst of cold wind hit them.

"You don't have to walk me. I'll be okay."

"What kind of gentleman would I be if I didn't?"

He took her arm, and before she could protest, he pulled her down the steps and across the bridge to her cabin.

Their breath spiraled in front of them as they laughed. Stopping at her cabin door, they exhaled.

"It really is cold out here."

She turned and took his hands. She looked so beautiful under the twinkling lights. A breeze brought her hair across her face before returning it to her shoulder.

"Which is why you should come in, don't you think?" She cocked an eyebrow.

"Are you sure? I mean…"

"You don't have to say it, Caleb. I don't want to think too much about this. We're having fun. That's what matters, right?"

He squeezed her gloved hands.

"Right."

Emma scanned her card, and the door beeped. She pushed it open and stood in the doorway.

He followed her without hesitation.

Chapter Fifteen

Emma set her bag on the counter and began peeling off her coat.

"Just so we're clear, I don't want you to feel any way about this. We can just hang out, or sleep, or whatever—"

Her sentence was stopped by the presence of Caleb's icy fingers on her cheeks. "I have a feeling you and I are both overthinkers." He must've realized how cold his hands were, as he pulled them from her face and rubbed them together.

She tugged her other arm out of her coat, letting it fall to the floor. "I like to think of myself as a recovering overthinker. But yes, you're not far off."

"I know it's early for New Year's resolutions yet, but I think mine is going to be to think less and do more."

"Good. Let's *talk* less, too." Before she could lose courage, she arched up onto her tiptoes, bringing their mouths together.

Some small part of her worried that their earlier spark had come from the fact that it'd been so long since she'd kissed anyone but Davis.

Newness, and all that.

This kiss proved her worries were unfounded. He tugged her closer until there was no space between them.

Even her overactive brain had no choice but to quiet as they kissed.

She brought her hands to his chest. How long they stood like that, intertwined, she would never know. It could've been five minutes or two days.

When he eventually pulled away, she emitted a little gasp. He cupped her chin. "I know we were just saying that we were going to stop overthinking, but I do think we should address the elephant in the room."

Emma's eyes shifted from side to side. "I was unaware of any elephants, but okay?"

He smoothed his thumb over her cheek and took a step back.

"I kind of need to know *what* this is. As I mentioned, I'm not exactly the playboy type."

A jesting comment about him being more of a *Playgirl* type died on her tongue. He was trying to be serious.

"My reservation lasts until January first. It's December fifteenth. Let's say we spend the holidays together, and if that's all this is..." She trailed, desperately wanting to say she'd do anything for it not to be. "Then that's all it is. Are you on the same page?"

She wasn't great at playing it cool. Caleb could probably tell.

Something passed across his face. "So, no pressure?"

"None at all." She kept a bright smile on her face. "And no hard feelings either way, right?"

He exhaled. "Right. I feel better saying the words. Dodging the elephant has been hard for me."

She brought her arm around his waist. "Especially with it being imaginary, I can see how that would be especially difficult."

He gave her a half-hearted poke on the side. "As much as I'd like to stay here with you, the sledding competition starts obnoxiously early tomorrow. I should go."

"Oh." She tried not to let the disappointment show on her face. She wanted nothing more than to get under the warm flannel sheets with Caleb. But he was right. "I don't want to rush things," she murmured. "Especially if you have to be in full activities director mode tomorrow."

He snorted at that. "I doubt Sabrina or Brandon will allow for that. I fully expect one of them to be there in the morning. But I agree." He swallowed. "About not rushing."

She arched up, bringing her cheek against his. "Then you should go now while you still can. Because otherwise, I'm going to change my mind." She tilted her head, so they were eye to eye. "And there's really no talking to me once my mind is made up."

His chuckle was warm against her cheek. "That sounds oddly threatening, but I get what you mean."

They shared a quick kiss. "I'll see you at sledding, then?"

"After I hit the breakfast buffet, you've got it."

He opened the door. "See you then, Em."

He slipped out of the door. It latched automatically behind him.

"So, we're at nicknames now," she mused to herself. She kicked off her shoes and fell back into bed, smiling.

* * * *

The only hill worth using for the sledding competition was in front of Sky House, so Caleb spent the early hours of Sunday morning clearing the section of the parking lot where the sledders would finish their run.

Then, he had to climb the steep set of stairs to the top and spread salt on the slick steps.

Usually, he'd find this sort of work monotonous. But given his good mood, he found himself humming as he stacked sleds. He and Emma were on the same page. It was time to stop overthinking and have some fun.

"Is that birdsong I hear?" a voice called behind him. "Because that couldn't be my crabby brother, whistling while he works."

He half-turned to face Sabrina, dressed for the ski slopes, even though Sky House was not a ski resort. *Yet.* Brandon and Sabrina still had dreams of expanding, but that dream wasn't within reach right now.

"First of all, I was humming. Secondly, you're welcome to set this up. It's a pain in the ass. Literally. I almost wiped out twice as I was de-icing the stairs."

Brandon came behind her, dropping another set of metal sleds on the other side of where Caleb stood.

"We appreciate your help, Caleb. Even if my wife may not say it directly, we do."

"Stop speaking for me, *husband*," Sabrina said. "Of course I appreciate Caleb's hard work. That's why I'm here! To help."

Brandon laughed at that. "You're here because the biddies were talking about what a hustler Emma was at bingo. Then they got to talking about how you and Emma left together."

"And now you're up here, in twenty-five-degree weather, humming as you work."

"What are the criteria for entering the biddies, do you know, Brandon? I don't think there's a firm age limit since they brought Eleanor in, and she's not even fifty. Because I think it's time Sabrina got an application."

She gave him a half-hearted slap on the arm. "Inez was fixing to put on her boots and come get the details herself. So, you should be glad it's me, not her."

"I'd be happier if it were neither of you," he said.

"It's nice to want things," Sabrina said sweetly.

His glare quickly lessened when he caught Sabrina's smile. She might tease him, but it came from a good place.

Most of the time.

"I like Emma. She likes me. It's nothing serious. She's going through a bit of an upheaval in her personal life. It's more than just her ending her relationship with her ex. But that isn't my place to discuss."

Brandon and Sabrina exchanged a glance. "Then there's you, divorced and doing a whole lot of nothing. You deserve to have some fun, brother. I'll try and get the biddies to back off."

Brandon scoffed at that. "Good luck."

"The toy drive starts this week, so they'll have to be back in town for that instead of trying to hustle our guests out of money."

"Ugh, I hope they're not still considering me for Santa," Caleb said.

"Don't hold your breath," Sabrina said. "But I'll tell them you're too busy here to help."

"I thought I heard them talking about a sexy Santa calendar. Carlos as the cover boy, you for Mr. March?" Brandon said.

Carlos was the second-in-command at Ellis & Daughter. And, despite getting married last summer, he was still something of a town heartthrob.

"That they consider me in the same league as Carlos is kind of flattering. But I'd appreciate any intervention to keep me here."

"I'll keep that in mind." Sabrina checked her time on her smartwatch. It's almost time to rustle everyone up for the competition."

"What are the rules, again?

Brandon shoved a stopwatch at him. "The fastest one down the hill wins. No accelerants added to the bottom of the sleds." He pointed to the sleds' aluminum bottoms.

"Like what, cooking oil or something?"

Sabrina laughed. "You'd be surprised how competitive people can be. Especially for a free dinner at the lodge."

Caleb glanced to where people were starting to emerge from the lodge building. "As long as no one breaks a hip in the process."

"Oh, we won't start until the Falling Leaves Fire Department and EMTs are here to oversee the situation." Sabrina raised her hands over her head. "Over here, everyone! Let's get this party started!"

Emma was at the front of the pack. She wore a bright pink snowsuit with a silver jacket on top. She looked around as if she were eying up the competition.

"You look like serious business," Caleb said once she was in earshot.

"I have a surprisingly strong competitive streak. You saw that last night at bingo." She motioned to her snowsuit. "I knew I was right for bringing this. Everyone else looks like amateurs."

He snorted at that. "Well, I know who I'm putting my money on, then."

She grinned up at him. "Good to know I have the betting man's favor." Their eyes met, and she brought a hand to the crook of his arm. "Hi."

Just the way she said that straightforward phrase had him smiling from ear to ear.

"Hi. Did you sleep well?"

She took a step toward him. "Not really. Mainly because I was excited to see you."

Before he could respond, Sabrina's voice came booming over a megaphone. "All right, everyone! Line up, then it's time to sign waivers and hear the rules!"

"Where the hell did she find a megaphone?" Caleb asked.

At the same time, Emma said, "Waivers? Should I be worried?"

"For a sledding champion such as yourself? I wouldn't worry."

Emma ended up being fourth in the lineup. Unfortunately, the competition lasted all of twenty minutes before those waivers came in handy. One of the guests landed sideways in the parking lot and fractured their wrist as they braced their fall.

Sabrina and Brandon worriedly took off to tend to the guest. Everyone else wandered off. No one was interested in becoming the next one with an injury.

Clearly, this was an event that wouldn't be staying on the schedule after this year.

"Guess the first annual Sky House sledding competition is a bust," Caleb said.

"And I didn't even get a chance to go for glory. How disappointing." Emma brought her gloved hands to her face. She mimed wiping tears away.

"You're a champion here" — he patted his chest — "where it counts."

She let out a raucous laugh. "Okay, smart ass. You're missing out, not seeing my sick moves. That's all I'm saying."

"I'll take your word for it. Hey, do you want to get a hot cocoa to warm up? I've been out here for hours, and I'm about to turn into an icicle."

They turned toward the lodge. Emma looped her arm through his. "I heard the biddies talking about us. We're hot news, apparently."

"It doesn't take much to excite them. Are you okay with them talking? I mean, they can be a little judgmental."

She shrugged. "Let them talk. We're grown folks who aren't doing anything wrong."

"Amen to that," Caleb said.

She tugged on his arm. "Normally, I don't like being in the spotlight. But just this once, I'll take it. If it means I get to spend time with you."

Caleb's breath danced in front of him as he gazed down at Emma.

"Ditto, Em."

Chapter Sixteen

Emma spent the afternoon in a paint-and-sip class run by Sabrina. She'd hoped to see Caleb, but he was still dealing with resetting the front of the resort after the sledding competition.

Emma, Sabrina and a group of older ladies had set up by the large fireplace in the lodge. The fireplace, decked out with Christmas decorations, was the inspiration.

Aside from her easel, Emma had a hot toddy and her art supplies. She'd chosen the gouache paints because she loved the watercolor look.

She took a sip and appraised her work. She wouldn't call herself an artist by any means, but she'd always liked to scribble and doodle. Recently, she had turned to sketching, but she didn't take it too seriously.

As she mixed up paints, Sabrina rolled her chair in place next to her. "Well, damn. You've got a lot of hidden talents, Emma. That's beautiful."

Emma blushed. "I guess I'm kind of an arts and crafts gal. Well, I used to be."

"Why are you using past tense?"

Davis was not the type who would've allowed paintbrushes to be washed out in his kitchen sink. So, she'd stuck to watercolors at first, then worked on lettering, before the inspiration had eventually left.

"Eh, my ex keeps his condo like a luxury car showroom. No personality or warmth allowed." She brought her paintbrush to add golden flourishes to the decorations around the fireplace. "He did give me my own office that I could do whatever I wanted with." She dabbed her paintbrush in the palette once more. "It was in the hall closet, but it was better than nothing." She turned to find Sabrina wearing a disgusted expression. "I know how that sounds. But I do have a space of my own. Well, I did."

Sabrina rolled her chair back slightly. "I heard you were looking at the empty spot next to the Ellis & Daughter office."

Emma set down her brush and gave her painting the critical eye. "Word flies fast, huh?"

Sabrina chuckled. "Small towns. No, but Caleb told me how you'd always wanted to open a stationery store. I can see now that you've got an artistic flair. Did you know there's an unused second floor in the space? It'd be perfect for something like this. There are a lot of talented people in Falling Leaves. Lots of clubs that *aren't* excuses to get together and gossip." She nodded toward her mother and Inez, bickering over their joint canvas.

Emma could see it. She'd always wanted to teach hand-lettering. Or art journaling. She could bring in artists to teach townsfolk and tourists alike.

Then, the reality of starting a business when she had no source of income would set in. It was a pipe dream, nothing more.

"I love that idea. But I'm not sure if it's a realistic dream."

A waiter stopped by to drop off another hot toddy.

"Why do you say that?" Sabrina passed their empty cups onto the waiter's tray.

"Well, I currently have no job, no place to live… I think I have other priorities to sort out first, you know?"

"You do," Sabrina said softly. "It's just a thought. That space has been vacant for months now. And there hasn't been much interest, given that it's such a narrow space downstairs. So, there's no rush."

Emma took a sip of her drink. With just a few words, Sabrina had helped solidify this dream of hers into something tangible.

Sabrina chuckled. "You're thinking about what I said, aren't you?"

Emma was, but she was also thinking about Caleb, which felt a bit weird to discuss with his younger sister.

"You do have a persuasive way about you."

She rose to her feet. "That's a nice way of saying I'm pushy, but I'll take it." She squeezed Emma's shoulder before moving on to the next guest.

Emma returned to her cabin before dinner. She and Caleb had tentative plans to attend the Sunday night movie in the lodge's small theater. Even with the hustle and bustle of the holidays, Sundays were a slower night.

Weekend guests checked out that morning, and there was a lull before mid-week guests arrived. Few were like Emma, who stayed the entire holiday season.

She set her canvas in the corner of the room and regarded it in the soft glow of the Christmas lights. She'd always been harsh on herself, but she had to admit that she was talented at pretty much any art project she tried. She just wasn't sure that translated into running a crafty business. What did people say? Don't monetize your hobbies, or you'll end up hating them.

She rifled through her wardrobe to find the perfect casual yet pretty outfit. She pulled out a cozy sweater and leggings and tossed them on the bed.

Her phone chimed with a text. She reached for it and groaned. The message was from Davis.

Hey, do you have a minute to talk?

No, she most certainly did not. After all, what did they have to talk about? He'd given her the deadline to get her things out of his condo. She'd replied to that with a thumbs-up reaction. An acknowledgment without further comment.

They didn't have anything left to talk about. As she was debating a reply, another text came in.

I'll give you a call tomorrow. Have a good night.

She groaned and tossed her phone onto the bed. She immediately began to dread the conversation.

Then she remembered they were no longer together. She didn't owe him anything other than moving her things out of his place. She'd even pay to have it cleaned as a thank-you. After all, she could never have afforded to live in his swanky building on her own.

But that was it. She'd broken things off, and he'd taken the ring and left her here. There was no coming back from that.

* * * *

"Looks like movie night might be a bust." Caleb closed the door to the popcorn machine.

"Most of our guests are older," Sabrina said. "We always like to have activities available if anyone is bored in their room. But it's not uncommon to have events with zero turnout."

"I know you keep track of these things. How long should I stay to see if a guest turns up?"

"Well, one guest is for sure coming," she said.

Caleb rifled in a box for more popcorn buckets. "Emma."

"Yes. She and I had a nice chat this afternoon at the paint-and-sip class."

He groaned. "Don't go scaring her off. It's only been a few days."

"It sure feels like a lot longer, doesn't it?"

He set the popcorn buckets down harder than he had to. "You need to butt out, biddie-in-training."

Sabrina put her hands in the air. "We didn't talk about you at all. We were talking about the space next to Ellis & Daughter. Wouldn't it be a perfect stationery store and artist space? I don't think we've ever had a stationery store in town, have we?"

"We haven't, far as I can recall. I think it would fit in well, if that's something Emma wanted to do."

Sabrina turned to look at her watch. "I need to get out of here. We have an end-of-the-year meeting with the Westmores tomorrow at the Pumpkin to go over Sky House's P&L statement."

He knew that, like many small businesses, Sky House had a rocky first year. More loss than profit. But they were hoping to enter year two stronger than ever.

"I can take it from here. I'll see you tomorrow."

"Don't forget we've got the Ellis & Daughter company Christmas party Tuesday night in the private dining room. You can bring Emma, if you want."

He rolled his eyes. "Goodnight, Sabrina. I'll see you tomorrow."

She snickered and walked away. He turned back to the popcorn machine, inhaling the aroma of buttery goodness.

Soft footfalls at the door had him on alert. "I thought I told you to go home?"

"Did you?" Emma's voice was quiet.

He turned to find her in the doorway, a somewhat bemused look on her face.

He cursed under his breath. "Sorry, I thought you were Sabrina. She's been acting like a biddie-in-training lately."

Emma's cheeks were still red from the cold. "Hmm, does that mean I should ignore her invitation to the Ellis & Daughter company Christmas party?"

He slapped his hand against his forehead. "I swear to god, she's getting coal in her stocking. Sometimes I have to remind her that it wasn't so long ago that it was her and Brandon's romance the biddies were intruding on. Funny how quickly she's forgotten."

Emma grinned. "So, you're saying the Coffee & Knitting Society moonlights as a matchmaking agency?"

"Among other things. Ready to watch the movie? There's a few to choose from." He pointed toward a large binder of DVDs balanced on the back of one of the seats.

"I'm feeling adventurous. You choose."

He gently nudged her in the side. "Are you sure? My favorite Christmas movie of all time is *Ernest Saves Christmas.*"

Emma's laugh echoed in the small, cozy space. "Okay, maybe I'll choose then."

"I can't say that I have the most highbrow taste in films. I'm sorry."

She clicked her tongue against her teeth. "I guess that's fair. You must have at least one flaw."

Before he could reply to that, she whipped out a DVD and handed it to him. *"White Christmas.* Appropriate, since it's Christmas and we're at an inn...well, a lodge, I guess."

He blinked at Emma before taking the DVD from him. "To be fair, I have several. Flaws, that is."

"Leave the toilet seat up? Forget to take the trash out?"

The DVD loading screen appeared. Caleb reached for the remote to lower the volume.

"The toilet seat is almost always in its upright position unless the girls are staying with me. I can be a little forgetful. My ex-wife would sometimes call me the doddering professor. I'd leave little piles in my wake. But I'd clean them up eventually."

"I'm kind of messy, too. Or, at least I used to be, before I moved in with Davis. He had a cleaning woman come twice a week."

"I like a little bit of chaos and clutter in my house. A good thing, since I have kids."

Emma reached for a popcorn bucket. "Is it weird dating when you have kids?"

"Is it weird dating someone who has kids?"

Emma shook her head. "I mean, I guess it is? If dating is what we're doing? Davis never wanted children, so I knew that was never going to happen for me."

He took a step toward her. "I'd call this dating. But what about you, Em? Do you want kids?"

She played with the bucket. "This is kind of a heavy conversation to have right before a Christmas movie."

He took a step back. "I'm sorry. I guess it's just a natural conversation around here. Most of the women I've seen since the divorce either have kids or want them."

She turned away from him to scoop popcorn into her bucket. "I guess you could say my upbringing soured me on the idea of having children. I've seen what can happen when kids are unwanted."

He couldn't imagine how Emma must have felt as a child, being abandoned by her mother, losing her grandmother, and being shuffled through many foster families.

"That said, I'm not a child hater or anything. I know that's a common stereotype that comes alongside being child-free. I'm not even sure that's exactly what I am, anyhow."

"It's understandable if you were," Caleb said.

"I've always liked kids. My foster sister Aniyah has kids. I'm their godmother. So that's not an issue."

Caleb cleared his throat. "Thank you for being honest with me. I'm sorry if I ambushed you."

She dipped her hand into the popcorn bucket. "You didn't. You're right—this is a natural conversation.

Even if this is a fun holiday fling, we can still know who each other is outside of this place, right?"

She wouldn't quite meet his eyes. He had to wonder if she was feeling the same thing—that they were fooling themselves if they thought this could ever be just a holiday fling.

"How about we turn on the movie?" She shoved a handful of popcorn into her mouth.

Conversation over. Hopefully, he could recover the night before it took another awkward left turn.

A small bit of popcorn found itself on her cheek. He reached over to brush it away.

"I'm glad to get to spend another night with you, Emma. I can't tell you how happy these last few days have made me."

Then, taking a page out of her book, he shoved a handful of popcorn into his mouth, preventing further conversation.

Emma chuckled. "I see how it is. Come on, let's get the singing and dancing shenanigans started."

Chapter Seventeen

She wasn't sure who'd dozed off first. Emma jolted awake sometime after the movie booted back to the DVD menu screen. Caleb was knocked out in the recliner next to her. His blanket had slid off his lap and now lay pooled around his feet.

She'd felt nervous at the beginning of the night, given the heavy turn their conversation had taken. But if her answers had thrown him, he hadn't shown it. They'd chatted off and on during the movie, until they'd both drifted off.

Perhaps it was her upbringing, but sleep had never come easily for her, especially not in a strange place, and with a — not so — strange man.

There really was something special about Caleb.

She took a moment to gaze at him. He snored ever so slightly, unsurprising given his position, with his head tilted back.

He looked so comfortable, she hated to disturb him. But she knew as well as anyone that once you passed thirty, sleeping in an unusual position would lead only to aches and pains come morning.

She pushed her leg rest down and tossed the blanket to the side. Then she quietly approached Caleb. She gently placed a hand on his shoulder. She paused, waiting to see if her touch would wake him. He didn't as much as stir.

"Wake up, sleepyhead."

He jolted awake so suddenly Emma took a step back so they wouldn't knock heads. He sat up with a start and gasped out a breath. He dropped a hand onto his chest when his eyes landed on Emma.

"Sorry, the dad reflexes kicked in. Normally, when I'm woken out of a dead sleep, the words 'Dad, I threw up' are to follow. Then the world's worst scavenger hunt begins." His voice was all kinds of raspy.

She stifled a laugh. "Sorry. We've both had a long day. It's not a remark on present company that you fell asleep. Because I did too."

"I know, you fell first."

She laughed before she could stop herself. "You have no idea just how right you are about that."

He gave a gentle tug on her wrist, taking the breath out of her as he pulled her into his lap.

She let out a yelp at the sudden movement. But she didn't protest further when he draped an arm around her shoulders.

"You're going to have to expand on that statement."

"From right here? What happened to where I was?"

He draped his other arm around her waist. "I wanted you closer, is that a crime?"

She exhaled. "Hmm, I'm not sure of the jurisdictions in this here county, but I'm going to assume that it isn't."

He stole a quick kiss before prompting her to answer.

She brought her head to his shoulder. Nestled there, she'd never felt safer.

"On check-in day, I think I saw you before you saw me. I started mentally calling you the lumberjack."

"Because of my outfit, I'm sure."

She arched back to look him in the eyes. "And nothing to do with your resemblance to that handsome cartoon-man logo of a certain paper towel brand."

Even in the dim light, she could see his cheeks redden. "I thought we established that my resemblance was middling at best?"

"Oh my god, are you embarrassed? I'm so sorry."

She wasn't, not really. As far as cartoon logos went, there really weren't any better than the paper towel man.

"Well, if we're going to get specific, I noticed you as soon as you walked through the entrance. I thought to myself that maybe this event planner gig wouldn't be so bad. Then I saw Davis trailing behind you. I don't know why I'd assumed you'd be alone. Almost all our guests are families."

"Well, I'm alone now."

He brought his index finger to her chin. "I'm glad. Otherwise, the amount of pining glances I would've thrown your way by now would've labeled me as a stalker."

A sarcastic reply died on her lips as their eyes met. "Perhaps everything's worked out as it should, then."

The only answer he had for her was a kiss.

And oh, what a kiss it was. She inched closer to him, her arms thrown around his shoulders as he looped her in with an arm around her waist.

This was her idea of heaven. Funny how she hadn't known Caleb existed a week ago. Now, it was hard for her to imagine a life without him.

The projector screen clicked off, causing the two of them to jump apart. Emma nearly slid out of his lap before Caleb caught her.

"Well, that scared the bejesus out of me," he said.

She laughed. "If I have a new gray hair in the morning, I know what's caused it."

He brought his hand to her face. "Can I walk you back to your cabin? I wouldn't want you to get spooked again."

She exhaled. "I'll let you walk me as far as the door. Don't you need to help set up breakfast? It's already after midnight."

He cursed under his breath. "Thank you for remembering my schedule better than I do. You're right. Another time, then?"

She stole a kiss. "One where we don't have to rush."

"I'm off on Wednesday. Tuesday night's the party, if you want to come?"

"I do."

He drew her in close. "I don't want you to feel obligated, or anything. If you change your mind between now and then, Em…"

"I won't." She drew her hand down his bearded cheek. "But I appreciate the out, anyway. Come on, let's get out of here before I change my mind."

* * * *

As much as Caleb wished he could do nothing but spend time with Emma, he did have work to do. No activities to run—thank god—but there'd been a few urgent cabin repairs that were discovered prior to a large group's arrival.

He, Brandon, and Carlos were holed up at the rear of the property for most of Monday and Tuesday.

From the one or two times they'd crossed paths, Emma informed him she'd passed the time by going on another tour of Falling Leaves with Sabrina and other guests.

When he'd brought up the stationery store, she'd smiled and said she was hoping to get a look inside before the end of the week.

Caleb wasn't prone to daydreaming. He was far too practical for such a pursuit. But as he worked, a vision came to him. One of him and Emma, living happily in the town. Her running the stationery store, him....

That was where the fantasy stuck. He had plans to talk about his ideas for the business with his father in the new year. But even those were vague. He needed to carve out his own path. Be it the family business or returning to teaching.

There was also the issue of his children. While his daughters were quite young, he was hesitant about bringing strangers around them. As much as he'd felt a bond with Emma over the last week, she was only a step above a stranger to him. It didn't matter that it felt as though he'd known her all his life.

Still, the happy thoughts overrode the worries. This thing between them could be something. Especially if she was serious about staying in town.

"Yo, Caleb." Carlos' voice dragged Caleb out of his thoughts.

He snapped to attention, finding Carlos packing up his tools. "It's time to get changed for the party. You did remember the holiday party is tonight, right?"

How could he forget? Sabrina had reminded him that Emma would be joining them. She hadn't been scared off by his family yet. Hopefully this wouldn't send her running for the hills.

"Yeah, I remember. Is Yessica coming up?"

Carlos snorted. "My wife is already in one of the cabins getting ready. It was nice of Sabrina and Brandon to offer that to us."

Ellis & Daughter had only two full-time employees aside from the family—Carlos and their newest employee, Kayla. She was a design assistant who helped keep all the cogs and wheels moving. Without her help, it would've been impossible for Sabrina to juggle working between Sky House and the family business.

"That was nice of them," Caleb said.

"Although I heard your new girl is already staying here. I thought staff weren't allowed to date guests?" Carlos half-heartedly wagged his finger in Caleb's direction.

"Since I'm technically not a full-time employee, and my sister is eager to get me coupled up again, those rules seem to have been ignored in my case."

Carlos snickered at that. "I can't wait to meet her."

"Hey, don't you give her a hard time, too. The whole family seems to think she's…"

"Think she's what?" Carlos paused in the doorway.

He slammed the lid shut on his toolbox. "Amazing, I guess?"

"Oh no, you've got it bad," Carlos murmured before he ducked out of the door.

* * * *

His sister was annoying in many ways, but one of her good qualities was that she thought of everything. Before Caleb could wonder what he'd wear to the party, considering most of his clothes were still in his apartment in Falling Leaves, he'd returned to his room at the lodge to find clothes laid out on his bed and a note from Sabrina.

Wanted you to look your best tonight, big bro!

She'd added a poorly drawn winky-eyed emoji at the bottom of the page. He shook his head. She'd chosen a dark pair of slacks and a blue shirt. Not that he had much fancier in his wardrobe, but it was an outfit he felt comfortable in.

He found himself grateful for the dark slacks during the short walk from his room to the private dining room where the party was taking place. His palms were clammy as hell. Why was he nervous? He knew everyone in attendance. Hell, it wasn't even as though Emma hadn't met his family already.

He couldn't put his finger on why, but he felt different.

As he approached the dining room, music and laughter carried out into the hallway. Sabrina's raucous laugh greeted him as he walked into the room. She and Emma were in the corner, drinks in hand.

"There's the man of the hour!" Sabrina turned to Emma. "I hope this doesn't weird you out, but I picked out his outfit for him. I figured it was better than the lodge uniform or his ratty work clothes."

Emma grinned. "I don't mind, but it appears that Caleb does."

Instead of having an irritating conversation with his sister, he took a moment to take Emma in. She wore a pink dress embellished with tiny, glittery Christmas trees that twinkled in the dim light. Her dark hair was piled in an elaborate updo.

She was the most beautiful woman he'd ever seen in his life.

Emma touched her hair. "Would you believe that your mom did my hair? I mean, I didn't have much say in the matter, but I liked how it came out."

"I had to tell her to take it down a little bit." Sabrina brought her hands out to either side of her head. "You know mom loves her poufy hair."

Brandon called Sabrina over to the other side of the room, leaving Emma and Caleb alone.

She reached for his hand. "I missed you," she whispered. Before he could reply, she added, "But I've been having fun on my own, don't worry."

He squeezed her hand. "I hope my family isn't too much for you."

"No, they remind me of those last couple of years I had with the Hendersons before I left for college. The house was rowdy, but full of love."

"I'm glad you feel that way." Caleb worried about his sweaty palms—he pulled his hand away from Emma's. "Sorry, my palms are sweaty as all get out tonight. I don't know why."

"How about we get you a drink? The bartender makes a mean Screwdriver. Because, of course, the drinks are all construction themed."

"That sounds like a plan."

She stood on her tiptoes and kissed his cheek. "I'll be right back."

He watched as she maneuvered through the room, pausing to converse with the other guests on the way.

He couldn't have taken his eyes off her if he tried. Maybe Carlos was right. He was down bad.

Chapter Eighteen

Maybe it was the booze, but Emma couldn't recall a time when she'd laughed more. This rowdy little party was the opposite of the holiday parties her firm would throw. Or, god forbid, the ones she'd have to attend at Davis' work.

"Emma is the newest person here. It's only fair that she has to be the one to do shots. Last year, it was me," Kayla said.

"Hey now, I'm not an employee!" She paused. "What kind of shots are we talking here, anyway?"

That had the whole group roaring with laughter.

Caleb reached for her hand under the table. "Trust me, this is an offer you want to refuse."

"Too late!" Sabrina stood from the table and disappeared.

Emma groaned. "It's not nice to haze newcomers, you know."

"It's only one shot," Brandon said. "Each."

"Each?"

Before he could reply, Sabrina returned with a wooden board with several shots lined up on it.

She nearly tripped on the carpet, but somehow, all the drinks were unspilled when she set them in front of Emma.

"We can start with the grasshopper."

"Oh god, please don't," Kayla wailed. "I was puking green all night."

Sabrina ignored this outburst. "Then the eggnog shot. Lastly, there's the Polar Bear Snowshoe—the signature Sky House Christmas shot—made with the finest Virginia bourbon you can find."

Emma stared at the tiny glasses in front of her. Ordinarily, she'd loathe having this much attention on her. But tonight felt different.

She stood, reached for the first shot, and downed it, which elicited a cheer from the other guests. She repeated the motion with the other two before collapsing back into her seat.

"That's a girl, Emma!" Carlos gave her a round of applause.

"Oh god, that grasshopper shot is so gross." She stuck out her tongue and shook her head.

Sabrina whisked the shooters away and plopped a bottle of water onto the table. "That'll help keep them down."

She tried to crack the seal on the bottle, but it fought her. Caleb took it from her hands, and it snapped open.

"You didn't have to do that, you know. It's just a silly Christmas tradition."

She turned, finding his gaze already on her. It was the booze that had her considering hopping from her seat into his lap.

Thankfully, she wasn't that drunk. "It was fun. Something I haven't had a lot of lately." She took a long sip of water. "Until I came here. And met you."

She realized too late that all the conversation in the room had died down.

"Man, you small-town folks really are nosy, huh?" Emma said.

"You better get used to it," Brandon said. "Speaking as one former city kid to another, it takes some getting used to."

"Oh, you love it." Sabrina sat on the arm of Brandon's chair.

He gazed up at her. "You're right, I do."

They shared a kiss. Lainey reached for her purse and pulled out a handkerchief. "Oh, I just love seeing all of my kids happy."

Caleb blushed. "Mom, seriously. Don't get started on one of your sentimental journeys."

She waved her hand between Emma and Caleb. "A mother knows! I was right about these two, wasn't I?"

Emma placed her hand on Caleb's arm. "I think it's all happening a little fast, is what Caleb's saying. Right?"

The deer-in-headlights look dimmed. "Right. I haven't even known Emma a week!"

"Not to be a buttinsky, but me and your mom were engaged after a weekend," Greg said.

"When you know, you know!" Lainey said.

Caleb's arm tensed under her touch. "Caleb must be up early to help out with breakfast. Isn't Santa going to be in attendance?"

"I better not be getting stuffed into that suit," Caleb griped.

"Oh, it'll be me. We should probably head to bed too, darlin'." Greg gave Lainey's leg a pat.

"I'd call you both lightweights, but Emma's right," Brandon said. "He is still technically a Sky House employee. And I'm pretty sure one of the biddies arranged for kindergartners to come in for breakfast with Santa. So you'll need all the rest you can get!"

Caleb groaned but didn't complain as Emma led him away from the table. She felt surprisingly sober, given the drinks she'd had tonight.

They were quick with the goodbyes — thankfully, since Emma was aching to kiss him.

No sooner than the dining room doors closed behind him did she reach for him. "I apologize in advance if my breath smells like crème de menthe and bourbon."

He laughed. "Somehow, on you, I think I wouldn't mind."

He looped an arm around her waist, bringing her close. She let out a little yelp as he brought her off her feet. He lifted her as though she were nothing.

They stumbled a bit down the hallway until they reached the rear elevator. Caleb forced himself to put Emma down.

"My room is just upstairs. Or we can go to yours — ?"

She wasn't sure if she could wait another minute, let alone the time it would take them to put on their coats and walk back to her cabin.

The elevator could sense their urgency as it arrived within seconds of being called for. Once they were inside, Caleb gathered Emma into his arms again. But only for a hug.

"There's cameras," he whispered into her ear. "And you know my nosy-ass family will be checking them in the morning."

She laughed against his chest. "Thank you for mentioning that."

Their short journey ended, and they arrived at the second-floor staff quarters. Caleb's room was only steps from the elevator.

With one quick swipe of his key card, they were inside. He fumbled for the light switch. Emma kicked off her shoes and took a moment to look around the small space.

There was a simple twin bed, a couple of dressers, and a TV opposite the bed that looked like a leftover from the 1980s.

"The staff quarters are kind of low on the priority list. Sorry if it smells kind of mildewy in here. It kind of ruins the mood."

She grabbed the front of his shirt. "Not on your life. Now come on, already, Caleb."

She drew him in for another kiss, pulling him backward to the bed. It didn't matter if this place smelled like an old summer camp or that they'd have to find a way to fit on this little bed.

She was with Caleb. That was all that mattered.

* * * *

He wanted nothing more than to sleep with his body curled around Emma's. Given the twin-bed situation, though, that wasn't going to happen.

"You roll over once, and I'm going to be on the floor," Emma said.

He watched her as she dressed in the dim light. He was exhausted, happy and satisfied.

"Fair point. Are you sure you don't want me to walk you back?"

"No," Emma said. "You need to be up in four hours. I don't. I think I might get room service for breakfast and stay in bed for a while." She slipped her shoes on. "Just an FYI, in case you finish up early."

He grabbed her by the wrist and tugged her back onto the bed. "Don't give a man ideas."

She leaned forward, her hair cascading over him. "I'll try not to. Have a good day. I'll see you later today."

He drew her in for a kiss, but she ducked away before he could deepen it.

"We both know where that will go. And we're too old to stay up all night."

She brushed another kiss across his brow. He was asleep moments after she'd slipped out of the door.

* * * *

Because it was midweek, there were few activities to keep Caleb busy. Most of the guests were at the ski resort or doing their own thing during the day. Sabrina had him working on smaller repair projects around the lodge.

After checking the leaky roofs, he ripped out the shag carpeting from one of the last cabins to be renovated. He had his headphones in and was living the introvert's dream — working with no human interruption.

As he was working, a call came in from Olivia.

"Why, hello there, Romeo."

"Who are you calling Romeo? Has the high mountain air finally gotten to you?"

She laughed at that. "You seem to forget that your sister and I are still good friends. She sent pictures from last night. Emma is absolutely adorable, Caleb."

It was a world full of weird to have his ex-wife give her opinion on his new girlfriend…if he could call her that?

"Sabrina is earning her spot in the biddies, that's for sure," he groused. "I was going to tell you about it. For now, it's just a vacation thing."

He could hear the rustling of one of his daughters in the background. Caleb's heart broke open. Between Emma and his work at the inn, he'd been doing a great job of keeping his mind off how much he missed his kids.

"Who is that?"

"Poppy. She's had a bit of an upset stomach, so I've been up with her all night."

"Sorry I'm not there to help."

"You deserve your adult time, Caleb. And if you've met someone who you think might be sticking around, we'll figure out what to do with the kids, same as we did when Ashley and I got together. Does she have any kids?"

Ashley and Olivia had been friends before they'd gotten together. She'd been around the girls a few times. But she'd kept her distance until things became official.

"No kids. Says she loves them but doesn't really want any, which is fine by me."

"Interesting," Olivia murmured. "I think we're going to go back to sleep for a bit here, but I just wanted to tell you how excited we are for you. You deserve happiness. I'll talk to you later."

After she ended the call, Caleb's mind turned to the time of their divorce. It hadn't exactly been a surprise when Olivia had wanted to separate. The stress of raising two young children had exposed the cracks in their relationship. They'd quietly separated nine months before Caleb had initiated the divorce.

In that time, Olivia and Ashley had gotten together. He'd known things were over when he'd felt nothing but happiness for Olivia when she'd told him the news.

Thinking about Emma leaving, on the other hand, had his stomach screwed up tightly. He dropped back onto his heels and exhaled a long breath.

This was something good. He wouldn't let his anxious thoughts ruin it before it even started.

Chapter Nineteen

Emma awoke to the buzzing of her phone. She groaned, annoyed with herself for not putting her phone in do-not-disturb mode before she went to sleep.

She rolled over and grabbed it. As her muscles stretched, she let out a happy sigh.

Last night had really happened. And Caleb was perfect, of course. She smiled against her shoulder.

She tapped her phone, dismayed to see the incoming texts were from Davis. She hadn't checked her phone since before the party last night, so the texts spanned from around seven o'clock last night to just now.

Is there any way we could talk this out? I really miss you, Em.

Ten o'clock. *You're leaving me on read now, Em? Seriously?*

Two o'clock. *Emmybear, I miss you.*

Just now… *Please give me a call when you get this. I'm worried.*

She groaned and kicked the covers off. The last thing she wanted was to talk to Davis. As much as her sappy, stupid heart wanted to believe that he was finally waking up to how amazing of a partner Emma was, she was too skeptical about that.

More than likely, Davis was starting to realize just how Emma had contributed to his life in a hundred different ways. Making sure all the bills were paid. Getting his suits from dry cleaning. Arranging his personal appointments and the like.

She was a glorified secretary. She'd done it all — for years — because Davis did help to give her a life she couldn't have afforded on her own. Before they'd met, she'd lived in a shitty condo in Adams Morgan with two roommates. With him, she'd wanted for nothing. So, it had felt like an even partnership, oddly.

Her life with Davis had been a step above. But she wondered if she ever truly loved him. This string of messages confirmed that even if she'd once loved him, she no longer did. She picked up her phone.

I appreciate you reaching out, but there's nothing to talk about. I'll be back in the city the first week of January, and then I'll pack up my stuff and return my keys to you.

Three bubbles appeared on the screen almost instantly.

Please, Em. I just want to talk.

She would never forget the way he'd snarled at her when she'd ended things with him. Davis might have always been indifferent, but he'd never been cruel. She could never go back.

We can talk in person in January, but it won't be about picking up where we left off. That ship has sailed. Have a Merry Christmas.

With that, she muted notifications on his messages and threw her phone back onto the bed.

She refused to let her ex put a damper on her mood. She needed to get out of this room. She showered, dressed, then left to walk to the lodge for a late breakfast. She winced against the late winter sun before going back inside to grab her sunglasses. She kept them on even after she stepped inside. Had it always been this bright in here?

Or was she just painfully hungover?

The restaurant was nearly empty, given that it was closer to lunch than breakfast. Lainey stood at the host stand, wiping down menus.

"Did those shots come back to bite you this morning?"

"No, it's just particularly bright in here today. Must be all the windows."

Lainey chuckled at that. "It's a good thing you missed out on the breakfast with Santa, then. Those kids were all over the place. I know just what you need to cure your hangover."

"Did Caleb dress up as Santa?"

"Don't you think I would've mentioned it first if he had?" Lainey laughed. "His dad was on Santa duty.

Now go find yourself a seat. I'll put your breakfast order in."

Emma bristled slightly at Lainey's bossiness — but then she let it go. Unlike Davis' mother, who'd been a commanding matriarchal figure, Lainey meant well.

Besides, it's not as if Caleb hadn't warned her how his family was. She knew what she was getting into.

She nestled into a booth by the window, set her journal on the table, and pulled out a small travel watercolor set. The hazy sunbeams stretching across the dining room floor inspired her.

Lainey swung by with a mug of coffee. "Do you need a glass of water for your paints, darlin'?"

Emma produced a water pen. "Thank you for asking, but this does the job just fine." She squeezed the base, sending water pooling into the paint pan.

"Well, ain't that something. You know, the biddies and I are very into arts and crafts. Are those watercolors? Maybe you could teach us a class in the new year."

Emma reached for her pencil. "You know, I haven't decided one way or another if I'll be staying in the area. Everything is new."

Lainey smirked. "You're right. That was my assumption. I put your breakfast order in. I'll leave you to your art."

As Lainey retreated, Emma exhaled. Perhaps she did have a side of crankiness with her hangover. She was tired of people assuming they knew what her next move was. First Davis, assuming he could work his way back after a few texts, then Lainey.

Lainey's assumptions were harmless, but they grated nonetheless. For the first time since she'd left college, she felt like the path of her life was truly up to her, which wasn't as exciting as it should be. It was downright terrifying.

She shook off her bad mood and returned to her drawing.

As much as she hated to admit it, Lainey was right about breakfast. Something about a super greasy breakfast sandwich with pure maple syrup to dip it in did her queasy stomach and shitty mood wonders.

"How did everything turn out?" Lainey appeared as Emma pushed her plate away.

"I feel a lot better, thank you."

Lainey leaned over her shoulder to look at her drawing of the breakfast room. "You've got real talent, Emma. That's so lovely. You should start selling these drawings."

"I had an online shop for a little bit, where I sold my work, but it got too overwhelming to keep up with. Maybe I will in the future."

"That reminds me." Lainey slipped into the booth opposite her. "I was going to head back into town. I could get the keys to look at the potential space for your stationery shop, if you want?"

"Seriously?"

Lainey reached over and grabbed Emma's hands. "You'll find that there isn't much I can't do, darlin'. I'm in the habit of helping people's dreams come true."

"That makes you sound like something of a fairy godmother."

"What makes you think I'm not?" She slid out of the booth and squeezed Emma's shoulder. "Stay put. I've got to wrap up a few things before we head into town, okay?"

* * * *

Lainey made the forty-five-minute drive down the mountain pass in what felt like a moment. She was the epitome of Southern charm. Normally, when people pried into her personal life, Emma put up a boundary. She hated the pitying looks she'd get when she told people she'd grown up in foster care. They wanted to know the whole rigmarole of what happened to her parents, what she'd gone through…it was exhausting.

Surprisingly, Lainey didn't press for many details, except for one.

"So, you don't know any of your birth family?"

"I never knew my dad. My mom tried to stay sober, but eventually addiction won. My grandma raised me until her death. Then I went into foster care because there was no one to take over kinship care. I've thought about doing one of those online DNA tests to see if it drops anyone off my family tree, but I haven't worked up the courage to do it."

Lainey pulled her SUV into a prime spot in front of the Ellis & Daughter office and cut the engine.

"Well, darlin', sometimes family is what you make of it. I've been blessed with mine. Everyone's always welcome in the Ellis family."

A knock on Lainey's window spared Emma from answering. She wasn't sure how she would, anyway. Maybe she'd spent too long in the city. People here were just kinder.

Lainey unrolled the window and waved to the woman on the other side. "Hi, Tinesha. She's one of the biddies," she told Emma.

"One that doesn't get as involved in their schemes, I promise," Tinesha added. "I'm just here to drop off the keys. I'll pick them up from you tomorrow morning."

"Do you own the building?" Emma asked.

"No, Mayor Ford does. I'm his assistant. He's not a bad landlord if you want to stick around." She gave a wave. "Nice to meet you, Emma."

"I didn't tell her my name," Emma muttered.

"You should know by now, in a place like this, you don't have to," Lainey said.

It took Lainey some wiggling to finally open the door. "Here we are."

Lainey pushed the front door open. Then Emma noticed the floral stained-glass detailing at the top of the door. The late afternoon sun sent rainbow-colored sunbeams across the old wooden floor.

Lainey flicked on the lights and closed the door behind them.

Emma took a moment to breathe in the old space. It had that aroma that old buildings often did. Dust, layers of old paint, and the battered wooden floors mixed to give off a scent you either loved or hated.

Emma was the former. She inhaled.

She turned to Lainey. "What has this space been over the years?"

"Well, it was the running store until earlier this year when they moved to a bigger space around the corner. Then, before that, it sat empty for a few years. No one wanted to be next to the Weird Sisters' metaphysical shop two doors down." Lainey rolled her eyes at that. "As much as I love this town, sometimes the stereotypes can be true about some folks being closed-minded, you know?"

Emma only nodded as Lainey carried on speaking. "It was an optician's office and a candy store when my kids were little. It could use some fresh life in these old walls."

Emma ran her fingers over the long, battered, dark wood shelves running along the left wall. She could see displays of curated pens, pencils and art supplies, small gifts, cards — the mental list went on and on.

"You've got a faraway look in your eyes. Come, let's look at the space upstairs."

Emma followed Lainey up the stairs at the rear of the store. They were sturdy, having recently been replaced.

"Now this space is a little rougher," Lainey warned. "The shoe store just used it for extra storage space, so they covered up the windows. So, use your imagination."

She pushed open the door and flicked on the overhead light. Dust motes floated in the weak glow emanating from several bare bulbs hanging throughout the space.

Only two walls of the space were usable. There was a strange angle to the roof, and the windows jutted out beautifully. But that didn't leave a lot of workable wall space. The back wall was also slanted, with a sink and counter taking up most of the room.

But she could see the space transformed in her mind's eye. Tables for crafting along the window wall. Perhaps some cozy chairs for reading or fiber crafts.

It would work.

"I'll tell you that the biddies have been looking for a space to gossip and work on our knitting projects. We could be your first customers."

"Oh, I couldn't charge you," Emma said.

Lainey gave Emma's shoulder a squeeze. "Friends and family rate, of course. Besides, we're all business owners around here. We've learned that true friends are the ones who support you with their friendship and occasionally their pocketbooks."

Emma let out a small groan. "Pocketbooks, yeah. I don't want to let my dreams get too far ahead of me. I am unemployed, after all."

"Well, not to get too much in your business, but Caleb did say that this wasn't exactly a pipe dream for you. That you were smart with your money and had some savings."

"I do. I just honestly have...no idea how much this would cost. I've never run a business before."

"Well, like I said, there are several of us who can help. How about the first step is to see what the rent will be? Then we can figure out the rest."

There was something oddly reassuring about her use of *we*. As much as she didn't want to get attached to Caleb and Falling Leaves, she worried it was far too late for that.

Chapter Twenty

Caleb was surprised to find Emma in Falling Leaves with his mother. Even more so to find out that she was looking at the vacant space next to Ellis & Daughter with his mother of all people. He didn't have much time to ruminate over it, as his mother had requested his presence at an impromptu Ellis family dinner at his parents' house.

Apparently, after they'd stopped at the space, they'd gone to the grocery store and now Emma was making dessert.

A trifle of some sort, judging by the blurry photo she'd texted him.

He'd felt oddly on edge during the drive. Maybe it was memories of when his family had first met Olivia. His mother hadn't been overwhelmingly thrilled with her — being from Boston, with close-cropped hair, multiple earrings, and a nose piercing, she was about the furthest thing Lainey would've picked for a future daughter-in-law.

They'd always been cordial to each other, but some of the testiness remained. Especially after they'd had the girls. Olivia had told him more than once that she was glad they only saw his family a few times a year. She couldn't stand Lainey's parenting advice.

Of course, since the divorce, it had all changed. Now they were buddy-buddy. They had a common goal—the kids. His mother even went to Olivia and Ashley's place in Blacksburg a couple of times a month to help with babysitting when Caleb was busy with work.

As much as he loved his mother, he hoped that Emma hadn't been tormented by her business advice or that, god forbid, she'd inferred something about his relationship with her.

Whatever that was.

He'd about worked himself up by the time he rolled his truck in front of his parents' house. He parked on the street behind Sabrina and Brandon's SUV.

Lainey had requested he pick up a couple of bottles of wine from Sky House, so he pulled those out of the passenger side and made his way inside.

He made it about as far as the end of the driveway, where he was greeted by his dad and Uncle Gordon, and the alluring aroma of fried turkey. They'd set up the deep fryers adjacent to one of the streetlights.

Even at their big age, they were dressed alike, in tacky Christmas sweaters. To hear them tell it, they never did it on purpose. It was just 'twintuition'.

"I thought Mom banned you from ever deep-frying a turkey again after the incident of 2015," Caleb said.

His father chuckled. "What incident? A little bit of the siding on the back of the house melted off, that's all. Easy enough to replace for guys like us."

"Lainey insisted that if we were going to try again, we do it at the very end of the driveway. But I'm a little worried about the bushes. She'll kill us if we melt her Christmas lights," Uncle Gordon said.

"Will you two of little faith knock it off? I've got this handled. Now get inside, Caleb. Your mama is waiting for you," Dad said.

"And don't worry, we know how to put out a grease fire this time," Uncle Gordon called after him.

Not feeling particularly soothed by that thought, Caleb stepped inside. The house was almost as lively as it usually was. With Gretchen and Sebastian's boys running around, and everyone gathered in the kitchen.

The only ones missing were Poppy and Emerson. A wave of loneliness hit him. It'd been over a week now since he'd seen his girls.

Soon enough, they'd be back in the fold. It was important for them to know all the branches of their family tree, not just his. That slightly soothed the ache of loneliness.

"You look like a deer about to go on a date with a pickup truck." Sabrina approached him from the side and swooped the wine bottles out of his hands. "You all right?"

His eyes focused to attention. "Are you sure the lodge will be all right tonight, with all of us here?"

She cocked her head. "It'll be fine. There are no major events planned tonight anyhow. Nice way to evade my question, by the way."

He cleared his throat. "I'm fine. Just missing the girls."

She patted his hand. "I miss them too. Caden and Graham are hopped up on sugar." She gestured to where their nephews were dancing wildly in front of the television to one of those super-stimulating cartoons.

Lainey popped her head out of the kitchen. "There you are, Caleb. Have your father or uncle burned off their eyebrows yet?"

"Eyebrows were intact, as of two minutes ago."

Emma appeared behind Lainey, a smear of something red on her cheek. He exhaled a long breath. *God, she's beautiful.*

"I hope that's not blood on your cheek, Em."

She reached up to swipe a finger across her face. She stuck it in her mouth. "Nope. Raspberry jam. I'm almost done with the trifle — do you want to help?"

The kitchen emptied out as he followed Emma in. By the looks of the stove and counters, dinner was about ready — save the questionable turkey.

Emma had taken over one edge of the kitchen island with her trifle. She wiped her hands and looked up at him.

"It's not weird I'm here, is it?"

He exhaled. "Why would you say that?"

She gestured to him. "Your vibe is off tonight. I just want to be sure you're not weirded out. I mean, not that I can go anywhere. I can't imagine how much an Uber up the mountain would cost."

He brought his hand to her face, forcing her to look at him. "I know how my mom can be. She probably steamrolled right over you."

Emma began opening cabinets. "She did, a little. But we were talking about the space, and when I looked up, I was at your parents' house and in charge of dessert."

"What are you looking for?"

"Does this trifle dish have a lid?"

He turned, remembering where his mother kept them. She had them organized by shape and purpose. It took him a moment to locate the right one.

He handed it over to her. "I know how my mom is. And yeah, I'm not going to lie, it was a little weird. But it's not like you hid in her trunk or anything to get down the mountain. You had a reason for being with her in town."

Emma snapped her fingers. "Damn, there goes my idea for hitching a ride into town tomorrow."

She snapped the lid on the trifle container. Caleb opened the refrigerator door and the two of them groaned as they began to move everything around to make space for it.

"It's just been a while since anyone I've had a romantic connection with has been at my parents' house. And with my girls being with their mom, I guess I feel a little off tonight. It's nothing to do with you, I promise. The weirdness is all me."

They fit the container in the fridge and Emma closed the door.

"Thank you for being honest with me about how you're feeling. It's refreshing after my last relationship."

Before he could reply, his mother ran through the kitchen. "They over-fried the damn turkey; would you believe it? It looks like shoe leather."

She grabbed the trash can from under the sink and was gone again. Caleb turned to Emma.

"You sure my family isn't too crazy for you?"

She smiled. "Maybe a little, but I think I can manage it."

* * * *

They ended up having a 'sides-only' dinner, as Caleb's mom called it. Her trifle had gone over a treat. Or they were just being polite. Emma could never quite tell with the Ellises.

She was too new to be on the brunt of their honesty.

Toward the end of the dinner, she found herself in conversation with Sebastian. They had a lot to talk about, given that he had opened Loaved Up earlier this year. She discovered that he had a background in finance, making him a powerful ally if she decided to start the business.

If only she didn't have those niggling doubts in the back of her mind. She'd become used to the struggle throughout her life. Even during her relationship with Davis, she'd never completely ditched the feeling that her life could crumble at any moment.

She knew now that was probably why she'd stayed with him for so long. He provided a sense of security.

Still, this seemed too easy. Everything was falling together so quickly that she couldn't help but be skeptical. Especially as Sebastian went over the costs of opening a business.

"Emma, hello? Are you still in there?" Sebastian waved a hand in front of her face.

"Sorry, I checked out when you started discussing numbers with multiple zeros after them."

He laughed at that. "It isn't cheap to open a business, that's for sure. But if you're worried, I'd be happy to help run some numbers for you. Obviously, everything will remain confidential between us."

She was a bit like a dragon hoarding gold when it came to her savings. Looking at the numbers in her different accounts reassured her. She had a fallback plan. She'd never be dependent on anyone else again, if she chose to go the hermit in the woods route.

This venture would take up most of her savings. And what did she have for collateral for a business loan? *Um, nothing except my hopes and dreams.*

"What were you thinking about calling the shop? Just so I know what to refer to the project as in my paperwork?" Sebastian gazed at her, phone in hand.

"Yours Truly." The words came out before Emma even registered them. "Yours Truly Stationery & Gifts," she clarified.

Sebastian's smirk was very similar to Caleb's. "Well, all right then. How about you come back to town in a few days and we can go over a plan? I'll text you for more info in the meantime."

Emma's gaze carried across the room, where Caleb was tossing one of his nephews up into the air. Sebastian followed her gaze. "Hey, watch out for the ceiling fan!"

Caleb set Graham onto the floor. "Sorry. You know how I can get."

Emma realized then that she did *not* know how Caleb could be. She'd only known him for a week. Nervousness bubbled up inside her.

Sebastian shook his head. "Does that sound good?"

Emma blinked slowly, trying to keep the creeping panic out of her eyes.

"Sounds like a plan."

She'd be a fool to at least not consider this option. After all, it wasn't like she had much of a life waiting for her back in DC.

Chapter Twenty-One

The closer the days drew to Christmas, the busier Caleb became. In addition to running breakfasts, he arranged guest shuttles to the nearby ski resort, cookie decorating competitions, present wrapping sessions, and this morning's event, one he hoped to wipe from his memory — Sweatin' with Santa.

Twenty of the fifty-five-and-over club dressed in their Christmas best and boogied down to upbeat Christmas songs. Of course, every one of the biddies had been in attendance. Thankfully, he hadn't had to lead the crowd — they'd hired a professional for that — but he'd found himself going hip-to-hip with several of the guests. Maybe the last two weeks had changed him, because he found himself actually *enjoying* it. Even with an itchy face from the beard glue, and an ache in his hips from all the dancing.

As the jolly exercisers moved on to drinks in the lounge, Caleb began putting the room back together.

"I hope you know that I have a video of you dancing with one of the friskier ladies. They should really learn to keep their hands to themselves."

He looked up to find Emma leaning in the doorway. He hadn't seen her much since the family dinner. He'd started to wonder if she was avoiding him, but then he remembered how busy he'd been. She'd also been preparing for her meeting with Sebastian, so she'd been holed up with her laptop.

He began taking off his beard. "I'm prepared to pay your ransom. What are your demands?"

She peeled away from the door. "Hmm, maybe should've thought more about this. I didn't think you'd pay a ransom. I was thinking dinner — you and me."

"You don't have to bribe me for that. I'd go happily." He set the damn beard down on the table with a slap.

"Well, now you tell me. I've always been a shitty negotiator." She smiled up at him. "I guess that was my way of saying I missed you. You've been busy, so have I."

He brought a hand to her face. "Sebastian told me you have a meeting with him today about the stationery shop."

"I'm oddly terrified. It's one thing to daydream about starting over and quite another to do it. I've been nervously checking my bank balance since I started working on this."

"Well, what's the saying? If you're not terrified, what's the point of trying?"

She leaned closer to him. "Did you make that up on the spot?"

His hand came to the small of her back. "I don't think so. I can go with you, if you want. I may not have the business acumen of my older brother, but I could be moral support."

"You're too busy for that."

He gestured around to the empty room. "That's the last event for today, until a special year-end bingo tonight. The biddies run that, and you've been unofficially banned. Once they make decrees like that, it's hard to get them to walk them back."

"I can't help that I'm a hustler." She leaned against him. The soft, floral aroma of her shampoo hit him straight in the feelings. He drew her closer before he brushed his hand down her back.

"I'll go with you as long as you promise to delete the incriminating video."

"There's no video. So, you'll come?" Her words were muffled against his shirt.

"Give me twenty minutes to finish cleaning up and change. You're meeting with Seb after closing, right?"

"I was hoping you'd keep your holiday attire on."

He laughed. "I'd never live that down."

Her eyes shone with mischief. "Fine, fine. Maybe later, though?" She gave him an oddly long wink.

He stumbled back with laughter. "I'm finding out all sorts of things about you today, Emma."

"I promise I don't really have a Santa fetish. I'll see you in a bit." She rose up to brush a kiss across his lips. "I'll meet you in the lobby in twenty."

* * * *

On the way down the mountain, Emma nervously scrolled back and forth through the questions on her laptop. Caleb kept one eye on her as he navigated the windy mountain roads.

"You're really taking this seriously, huh?"

She cut him a glance. "Well, yeah. It's a huge step if I choose to take it. Did you think this was all for show?"

"What? No. I guess I was just surprised to see you take to the idea so quickly."

She shut her laptop. "If you have something to say, spit it out, Caleb."

He exhaled. He hadn't meant to pick a fight. "I just meant that you want to be sure about this before you make any next steps. I know your life has gone through a huge upheaval in the last month. I want to be sure you're making the right choice."

She stowed her laptop in the bag by her feet. "I'm hoping that this line of questioning is coming from a place of concern, and not because you're having second thoughts about me moving to town." She turned toward the window. "Because as much as I've been having fun, this really isn't about you, Caleb. I'm doing this for me."

Heat flashed across his cheeks. How had he fucked this up so quickly? He hadn't meant to make her doubt herself. "That's not what I meant at all, Emma. I guess I'm just practical to a fault. This may not be about me. Fine, I get that. But you won't exactly be a stranger."

She folded her hands in her lap. "If you didn't want me to do this, you should've said so sooner."

This wasn't a conversation they should have while navigating tricky mountain roads.

Caleb pulled the van into a scenic lookout parking lot. "That's not what I'm saying at all. I'm just flustered. This is how I get. I just want to be sure you're making the right choice. I don't want you to have any regrets."

"I think the biggest regrets are the things you never did anyway. It's better to try and fail than regret not trying."

"You're right, and I'm sorry."

She took a moment to respond, her gaze focused on the view ahead of them. Even obstructed with fog and snow, the mountains were beautiful.

"You have to see it from my side. You came at me more than a little bit sideways, Caleb."

He reached over to grab her knee. "I realize that now. We don't exactly know each other as well as it feels. That's all this is. Ask Sebastian. He'll tell you about the two months it took me to decide where I wanted to go to college. I papered my bedroom with color-coded Post-its with the pros and cons for each school. In the end, I ended up going to Tech because I got a partial scholarship. So, all that overthinking was for nothing. Somehow, I still end up doing it, though."

She leaned back into her seat and kicked a leg up. "I'm not exactly the type to make decisions like this, either. But I'm kind of under the gun. I have no life to go back to in DC now. I need to decide what my next step is. I'd much rather choose adventure than a slightly different variation of the same old life I was living."

"I think we're both saying that we want you to be sure. I'm sorry if I got flustered and the words got all mixed up on the way out."

She reached for his knee and gave it a squeeze. "I appreciate you looking out for me, Caleb. Now, we should get moving. I have a feeling Sebastian doesn't care for tardiness."

Caleb chuckled as he put the van in gear. "You'd be right about that."

* * *

Emma couldn't shake off the weird feeling left by her conversation with Caleb. Even after he explained his very rational train of thought, she couldn't help but wonder if it was a roundabout way of telling her that he didn't want her hanging around after the new year.

She was probably reading too much into it. It's not like this would be her first time overthinking things. But when he didn't stick around for the meeting, instead saying he had to go next door to go over some documents for Ellis & Daughter, her worrying escalated. His reaction was proof that no matter how well they'd meshed since meeting, they really were just strangers.

Sebastian sighed as he scrolled through the financial information she'd prepared for him.

"Try not to look so dour, please," Emma said.

He took off his reading glasses and closed the laptop. "For someone with no background in business, I'm surprised at how good the first draft of your business plan is."

"Okay, that's positive. So why the sighing?" She wiped her sweaty palms on her jeans.

"I think you'll have difficulty obtaining a business loan. Meaning you'd have to drain your savings if you wanted to go this route."

Panic scratched up Emma's throat. She'd been a saver since she'd first realized that her belongings could be thrown into a trash bag at any time. Hoisted into the back of many social workers' cars, she'd realized no one would have her back except her. Knowing she had that money in the bank was how she slept at night.

"Not even with the monthly inheritance check I receive from my foster parents? Doesn't that count as income?" Ma and Pa Henderson had left an inheritance to all the kids. It was hardly enough to live on, but it was part of her monthly income.

"It's still not enough."

Her lower lip wobbled. Today really was about smashing the happy daydream she'd been living. She'd been stupid to think that she could achieve something like this on her own. Now what was she going to do?

"I guess that's that, then. Back to DC I go."

Gretchen stopped by to place a cinnamon roll in front of her before disappearing again.

"No one is saying that, Emma. You might need help that the banks can't provide."

She shoved the cinnamon roll into her mouth. "I don't exactly have anyone who can swoop in and save the day. It's just me."

"Well, that's not exactly true. We can help if you want us to."

She paused chewing. "Who's we?"

"Ever since we started Loaved Up, Gretchen and I have been interested in expanding the town's business district. We've been fortunate in life. We decided that if the right business opportunity came along, we'd consider investing."

Could he be saying what she thought he was saying?

She wiped at her mouth. "So, what are you saying? Business partners?"

Her mind trailed back to the strange conversation she and Caleb had had. Mixing business with Sebastian meant that Caleb would be part of her life regardless of their romantic status.

"Possibly. I can draft an agreement. Do you have an attorney?"

"I don't, but I'm sure you know everyone worth knowing in this part of Virginia."

"I can recommend a few impartial attorneys. In the meantime, why don't you think over what we've talked about here? I'll work on getting you a draft agreement by close of business Monday."

This all seemed too easy. Where was the catch? "Monday's Christmas Eve."

Sebastian shrugged. "It's one of the busiest days of the year for us. So, if I can't get the agreement to you by then, I'll be in touch, okay?"

She nodded. "I appreciate the offer, Sebastian. I'm not ready to give up on this dream just yet. I'm glad to know that it isn't quite a pipe dream after all."

He slid out of the booth. "I'm glad to hear it. I'll be right back so we can wrap up things."

She finished her cinnamon roll. This was good news—her dream was one step closer to becoming reality. So why couldn't she shake the feeling that she was about to make a huge mistake?

Chapter Twenty-Two

Caleb watched from the street as Emma and Sebastian wrapped up their meeting. He'd awkwardly puttered around the office, half-heartedly working on notes for his meeting with his dad. He felt as if he was chasing ideas around his brain—his thoughts more on what Emma and Sebastian were talking about next door.

It hadn't felt appropriate for him to sit in on that meeting. Especially after that awkward but much-needed conversation they'd had going down the mountain.

He'd half hoped a sinkhole would've appeared under the van during the drive. He'd meant to show his support for her decision. The word salad that had come out was more of a panic-stricken rant.

Why couldn't he be normal? Why did the words always find a way to get mixed up on the journey from his brain to his mouth?

They'd left on a good note, or so he'd hoped. As Emma looked up and caught him creeping under the streetlight, he wasn't so sure.

Her expression was clouded over. Perhaps the meeting hadn't gone well. Sebastian walked over to the door and unlocked it.

"Are you going to stand there like a stalker, or do you want to come in?"

He frowned. "I didn't want to interrupt."

"You're not. We're about done. Come in."

He followed his brother inside. Emma gathered her belongings, her expression still grim.

"You okay, Em?"

She looked up. "I have a lot to think about. I'm okay, though."

"Oh, before I forget, I do have the key to the space if you want another look before you head back. Caleb, you've never been inside, have you?"

"Um, once, when it was still the running store. I was more concerned with the shoes than eyeing up the space."

Sebastian produced the key. Emma stared at it. "How did you get it?"

He shrugged. "Mom may have forgotten to give it back to Mayor Ford the other day. I figured I'd hang onto it in case I saw him or you. Here. Take it. You should let Caleb see it."

Caleb reached for her coat on one of the hooks hanging by the front door. He inhaled that wonderful scent of her again as she pulled it on.

He kept his hands on her shoulders as she buttoned up her coat. Gretchen appeared from the kitchen and snuck a kiss from Sebastian.

"It looks like there's a wicked storm coming in," she said. "It should clear by morning. You two should stay in town tonight. I'll send you home with some food."

Caleb started to argue. In the afternoon, he had to help with the last-minute letters-to-Santa program for the kids.

"It'll be clear by the morning. Sabrina and Brandon are up on the mountain. I already spoke to them."

Gretchen was the quiet sort, but he knew when not to argue with her. "Okay, fine. If Emma's okay with it."

She turned the key over in her hand. "I'm more than okay with it. Let's go, Caleb."

It was only about a block and a half walk from Loaved Up to the space. Even he had to admit the town looked magical in the snow. Skaters twirled around the rink, lit up by Christmas lights of every color. Snowflakes danced in front of streetlights.

"You know, maybe this isn't such a bad place for a do-over. I came here for mine because I didn't have a choice. It's where I'm from. But I can see the charm on nights like this."

"It's like something out of a dream I didn't know I had until two weeks ago. Maybe that's why it still feels like lunacy that I'm considering taking this step. Especially after my discussion with Sebastian."

"Was it so bad? I'm assuming it's not impossible, if he gave you the key to the space."

"I'd need investment to get started. My finances aren't enough on their own. Especially since I don't exactly have a source of income right now."

He placed a hand on the small of her back as they crossed the street. "And Sebastian was open to the idea of investment?"

"It was his idea. I just feel... I don't know. Like it seems so presumptuous of me to ask this of him. Things never come this easily to me. I keep waiting for the catch."

A gust of wind blew down the street as they crossed. "It's not a gift. It's business. And trust me, I know my brother. If he thought your business idea wasn't solid, he wouldn't have even offered. He'd have looked over your proposal, given you a few tokens of his finance-bro wisdom, and sent you on your way."

They stopped in front of the space. Emma produced the key and held it in her gloved hand. It slipped out of her hand and rattled to the ground.

Cursing, she dropped to her knees to hunt for it. Caleb found it first, their gloved hands meeting.

She let out a laugh. "This is starting to get ridiculous, you know."

He handed the key over to her. "What do you mean?"

They both rose to their feet. Emma placed her hands on his forearms to steady herself.

Caleb didn't have a chance to worry over her words—her answer came in the form of a kiss.

What had gotten into her? Kissing this man under the flickering lightbulb in front of what could be the home of her future business.

It was time for both of them to stop overthinking. She broke away from his kiss. "Can we look at the space tomorrow? It's too dark to get a good look now, anyhow."

Confusion crossed Caleb's face. "What do you mean? I thought that's why—"

She cut him off with another kiss. This time, the confusion quickly faded. His arms came around her waist, cradling her close.

He broke the kiss. "Oh. I'm following you now."

Her breath spiraled in front of her as she laughed. "Took you long enough. Can we go to yours?"

The snow started to fall harder as they hurried the short distance to his apartment. Curious glances were cast their way by onlookers. She didn't care. Let them stare.

Maybe she was getting used to small-town life after all.

They stumbled up the stairs and into his apartment. He left the big light off, flicking on a lamp as they stepped inside. Paired with the flickering Christmas tree lights, the space had a cozy vibe.

They stamped the snow off their boots, unwound their scarves from around their necks, and unbuttoned their coats.

"I'm sorry, I can be a little dense sometimes." Caleb hung his coat on a hook next to where she stood.

She looked at him, his hair standing up on end. "I find it endearing in situations such as this."

He took her coat and hung it up. Their boots were toed off then she followed him down the hall to his bedroom.

She fell a step behind as they passed his daughters' room. Decorated for Christmas. An odd, worrying knot of anxiety appeared in her stomach. With all these decisions coming so quickly, she had to wonder, was she okay being with a man who had children?

This was just one more change she would have to adapt to if she wanted to move to Falling Leaves permanently.

Caleb flicked on the bedside lamp in his bedroom. It was then he noticed she'd fallen behind.

"Are you okay?"

She shook off her nerves. "Sorry. Sometimes I forget you have kids. It took me a moment."

He leaned in the doorway. "I know we've touched on it, but are you against me having kids? Because if you are, then this thing between us won't go further than this."

"I just don't want yours to hate me."

He chuckled at that. "If you're worried about a stepmother dearest situation, they're a little young for that. But we can take things slow, Emma. Olivia and I have already discussed that you'd meet them when we're all ready."

She worried her left hand over her right. "You've told her about me?"

He smiled. "She's still one of my best friends. But it's all platonic and co-parenting now. You don't have to worry about that. She's madly in love with Ashley. You'll probably be when you meet her, too. Everyone loves her."

She exhaled. "It's all so civilized. I guess for someone like me, who never really had stability in my life as a kid…it's equally refreshing and confusing."

"I think that's a great way to describe my family." He peeled away from the doorway. "Now, we can talk things out if you want. Or…?"

For the second time tonight, she cut him off with a kiss. "I'll take that second option, Mr. Ellis."

He drew her close. "Mr. Ellis is my dad. Or my uncle. Okay, this is getting weird. Enough talking about my family, please."

She wrapped her arms around his shoulders. He caught her around the waist, lifting her off her feet.

"Deal."

She kicked the door closed behind them. They fell back into bed, laughing.

Chapter Twenty-Three

Bright and early, they stood side by side in the empty space. Two days before Christmas, the whole town was sleeping in.

Except for them. Two weeks ago, he'd never met Emma. Now, he stood with her in the possible future home of her business.

The floor creaked under Caleb's boots as he moved around. "Can I tell you something crazy?"

"Crazy like 'I see dead people', or crazy like you like pineapple on pizza?"

He let out a laugh. "The answer to both of those questions is no." He turned toward her, extending his arms wide. "I can see a built-in on this wall for all the little things that could get lost in a shop like this. Trinkets, pens, stuff like that."

"Dark wood," Emma added.

"Exactly. Maybe wallpaper on the back shelves for a pop of color?" He laughed at himself. "I've been working with my sister and Kayla for too long. But seriously, I think that would look great, don't you?"

She drew an arm around his waist. "Maybe a long wood slab for the cash register? Built into the wall to save space?" She gestured to a blank spot of wall by the front door.

"I'm pretty sure I've seen the perfect piece of wood in the back room of my uncle's hardwood store."

She leaned against him. "I'm not crazy, am I? For wanting to do this?"

"If you are, then so am I. I can see it, Em. Yours Truly can be a real thing. You've got a good idea here."

She rested her head on his arm. "Well, if we two overthinkers agree, then it must be a good idea. We still need to convince Sebastian to invest."

He looked down, finding her already gazing up at him. "My brother wouldn't have mentioned it if he wasn't already seriously considering it."

She let out a giddy noise. "Let's get this key back to Sebastian, then. What time did you have to be back at Sky House?"

"Sabrina was vague. Just by sometime this afternoon to set up the letters to Santa event, then help set up for the choral concert in the chapel."

"Wait, there's a chapel?"

He laughed. "Yeah. It's not fully renovated yet. It's at the back of the property, surrounded by trees. It's beautiful."

"I must've missed that on the daily list of activities. But I've been a little busy."

Her phone buzzed in her coat pocket. She pulled it out, rolled her eyes, and shoved it back where it'd come from.

"Everything okay?"

"Yes. Come on, let's go back."

He wanted to inquire further, but she was already at the door, key in hand.

He followed her, offering his hand as they stepped onto the street. She looked up at the gray sky, with the sun making a feeble attempt at shining.

"You know, if I'm going to stay here, I guess I need to find someplace to live."

Caleb said nothing at first. He wasn't sure if she was dropping hints that she wanted to move in with him.

She gave him a nudge. "You should see your face! I wasn't asking to move in with you, Caleb. I guess with everything else, it just occurred to me that I'll need a place to stay."

He exhaled. "I didn't think that's what you were asking, but I wanted to be sure. Especially when it comes to Emerson and Poppy. That would be a big change for everyone. I want to be sure you understand what living with a toddler and a preschooler is like. It can be total chaos."

"Of course. Do you know anywhere that's renting? I mean, this isn't the type of town that has those luxury apartment buildings every two feet."

"I know of at least one apartment for rent in town. And Sabrina has a guest suite on the top floor of her house that she could rent out. She's only there about half the time, anyway. Do you like cats? She has two."

"I like cats just fine. So, you're saying I have options. That's good. Hopefully, the rent is a lot less than what I was paying in DC. "

Loaved Up came into view. Apparently, that's where everyone in town was congregating, as the line wove out of the door.

"I can only imagine what that cost," Caleb said. "I guarantee it'll be cheaper here."

"It wasn't as much as you think, mainly because Davis covered most of those costs. But he lives in one of those ultra-modern buildings with every amenity, so it was expensive. Even for DC."

"Well, here you'll find such amenities as running water and furnaces that may or may not go out in the middle of winter. But they're priced accordingly."

As they approached the line of people snaking outside his brother's bakery, several people turned to say hello. More than a few asked who Emma was. Including his annoying cousin, Dennis.

"So, a pretty lady moves to town, and you've already laid your claim on her? That's lame, Caleb."

He had to laugh at that. "About as lame as your pickup lines." He turned to Emma. "You should thank me for saving you from Dennis."

"Hey!" Dennis called after them.

Emma laughed. "I'll take the key inside really quickly so we can hit the road."

She brushed past the people at the door, assuring them that she wasn't cutting the line. He watched as she leaned over the counter to talk to Sebastian.

It was as if she'd been a part of their lives forever. It was time to stop overthinking and allow himself to relax once and for all.

* * * *

This was the right decision—Emma knew it in her heart. What was the worst that could happen? She'd fail as a business owner. Start over again. But this idea was worth the risk. She'd go to stationery and paper goods stores in DC and imagine herself running them, how she would stock the shelves, which artists' work she would carry, and how she'd dress up the shop for the holidays.

She'd never have considered a small town. She hadn't known places like Falling Leaves existed, and only a few hours' drive from the city. A place where dreams like hers didn't feel quite so impossible.

Once they returned to Sky House, she parted ways with Caleb, who had to get straight to work. She meandered through the main building before dropping down into a seat in front of the fireplace. She reached into her bag and pulled out her journal and travel watercolor palette.

Funny how this had quickly become a routine. She looked around, waiting for inspiration to take her. She'd already sketched the fireplace, along with the large Christmas tree. Perhaps the garland woven around the large wooden beams in the lobby?

She was terrible at sketching people. But she should probably work on that, especially if classes were going to be on offer at Yours Truly. She turned her attention to the myriad faces moving through the lobby. A few kids ran around their parents, decked out in their Christmas best.

Her eyes came to rest on the front desk, snagging on one familiar face. White-blond hair. Broad shoulders, slim build.

Oh, no. No, no, no. She rubbed at her eyes, finding that the sight in front of her wasn't just some unfortunate vision.

But she'd never be that lucky. Davis had returned just in time to ruin Christmas.

Chapter Twenty-Four

Emma thought about hiding, gathering her things, and escaping back to the cabin. The thing was, he knew which cabin she was staying in, so he could find her if he really wanted to.

She sighed and shoved her journal and supplies back into her bag. *So much for a relaxing Sunday morning.* Of course he'd ignored her when she said it was over. It wasn't as if they hadn't come close to calling it off before. He was a big fan of the grand gesture, but often lacked follow-through.

Looking at him now, she was more certain than ever that she'd made the right decision. He wasn't here because he loved her. No, he'd grown used to her presence in his life. All the little things she'd done for him to keep his life moving. Sure, he had a maid and an assistant at work. But they wouldn't have the keen eye for managing all the details of his life as she had.

Knowing him, he also saw marriage as a box to tick. They'd been together so long that she knew he would rather throw himself into the Potomac than get back on the dating apps again. Even though it was doubtful it would take him long to find a Capital Clone to fill her spot.

After all, it wasn't his looks that put women off.

She stood, and at the same time Davis turned to take notice of her. It was then she saw the bouquet of winter blooms nestled into the crook of his arm.

Oh, they were really doing this. He scurried his way across the lobby. She met him somewhere in the middle.

"Emma! There you are. The front desk person was telling me they couldn't deny or confirm that you were here." He rolled his eyes at the poor desk clerk before making his way across the lobby.

Of course they'd caught the attention of several of the people milling around in the lobby. Including two of the women she recognized as being part of the biddies. *Great*. This news would spread faster than a wildfire.

Davis came to a stop right in front of her. At least he had the good sense not to try to kiss her.

"What are you doing here, Davis?"

He offered her the flowers. She took a step back. "Come on, you can't seriously think this would work."

He cast a glance around the room. "Is there somewhere we could talk privately? Your cabin, perhaps?"

From behind them, someone cleared their throat. She found one of the biddies opening the door to the lounge.

Sometimes, their meddling came in handy.

She murmured her thanks as she passed the woman. Davis followed her into the dark lounge. She paused to flick on the overhead lights, which buzzed on one by one. Once the door shut behind him, he thrust the flowers into her arms.

"I feel ridiculous carrying those around."

She slammed the flowers onto the bar top. Petals scattered to the floor. "I would've thought you would feel ridiculous driving all this way. You had several hours to think this over on the way here. I was clear in my last text, Davis. We're done."

He started to roll his eyes but stopped. "You can't be serious, Em. What are you going to do? You have nowhere to live and no job. What are you going to do, stay around here with these hillbillies?"

He knew all the soft spots to poke at. He'd told her once before that no one else could ever give her the stable, comfortable life that he could provide for her. Knowing her upbringing as he did, it made the whole charade seem that much more cruel.

She narrowed her eyes. "So what if I am? It's none of your concern."

To that, he only shook his head. "Fine. I didn't want to do this, but you're not exactly giving me a choice."

She had no time to consider that thought. He reached into his jacket pocket and produced an envelope. "Here."

The envelope was pale pink, with a floral motif in the corners. "Did you take that from my office?"

"Where else am I supposed to find an envelope? You have an abundance of all that paper crap."

Paper crap. In those two words, he showed how little he cared about her.

She snapped the envelope out of his hands. She tugged it open with her index finger. Inside, she found a two-page invoice. Printed on both sides, it was a monthly record of their time together and the expenses he'd paid for.

"What the hell is this? A bill?"

He shrugged halfheartedly. "I did cover most of the expenses. If you want to break the engagement, I'll be expecting repayment."

"Oh, for fuck's sake, Davis. Are you serious? Charges for gas for picking me up from work? I paid my share of the expenses."

It was true that he had paid the mortgage, but she had also paid for utilities, parking—for a car she didn't even drive—and other miscellaneous expenses. His income was nearly double hers.

Of course, they'd never put anything in writing because why would they? They were in a serious relationship.

Emma's cheeks burned in shame. "I thought we agreed—"

"Well, it was never in writing, was it? I can and will sue you, Emma. There are legal precedents for this type of arrangement, even in the absence of a formal contract. You should know I keep immaculate records. It won't be hard to prove."

She slammed the papers onto the nearest table. "Do you even hear yourself? This is bonkers."

"I had a feeling you wouldn't come back. I figured it couldn't hurt to ask. Even though I doubted you would come to your senses in this garish Christmas wonderland. And if you said no, which you have—at least I could serve you with notice. I'll send you an updated invoice with just those charges. Because hey, I'm nothing if not a nice guy, huh?"

She flipped to the second page to see the total. Even removing the ridiculous fees, she was still looking at a bill of over ten thousand dollars. A third of her savings — already accounted for to start Yours Truly. Dread sank in her stomach like a stone.

"What about the utilities and expenses I paid? Or that I returned your stupid ring?"

He reached over her shoulder to tap a line on the printed spreadsheet. "Factored that into the equation. The ring was a gift, so that was not factored at all. This is what you would owe after considering those figures, with minimal interest."

She folded the paper up and shoved it back into the envelope. "Sue me if you want. I don't care. It's a he said/she said claim for small claims court anyway."

"It'll be a hassle, though, won't it? Coming back and forth to the city, paying an attorney… It's just easier if you pay now."

This smug fucker. He didn't need the money. This was punishment for her being the one to end things.

"I'll be back the first week of January to get my stuff. Don't think I won't be doing inventories of my own."

"Whatever you say." He turned toward the door. "Hey, you know what? I'll give you a fifty percent discount if you pay me by the new year. It'll be good for both of us, huh? Start the new year fresh?"

She reached for a heavy marble coaster and debated throwing it at his head as he made his way to the door. That would accomplish nothing, so she settled for crumpling up his stupid invoice.

A string of expletives slipped out of her. She slammed her hand against the edge of the bar. She'd been so sure about starting a new life in Falling Leaves. She'd spent long enough with Davis to know he wasn't the type to be slighted. It wasn't about the money for him. It was about reminding her who was really in charge.

She exhaled a breath. Tried to keep the anxiety from hovering over her head like a thundercloud.

But the rain fell, anyway, so much for her mountain town fantasy.

* * * *

The Falling Leaves High School chorus was never going to win any state competitions. Even with the perfect acoustics in the chapel, there were far too many flat notes for Caleb's preference.

He tried to tune out the choir as he wove Christmas lights around the ends of the pews. He was desperate to get out of there and to see Emma again. He felt they were now on the same page. She was moving to town — but to follow her dreams, not for him. It could be a little insulting if he thought of it that way, but he was glad for it.

He was the icing. The town and the business were what she was really coming there for. So if, god forbid, this thing between them didn't work out, there would be no harm done.

In theory, anyway. He couldn't imagine her right next door and not being his.

Emma's enthusiasm for her business only encouraged him to push his father for change in the new year. Ellis & Daughter would stay mostly the same, but they would add sustainable builds and interior design to their repertoire. Kayla was working on getting her associate's degree in design and was on target to graduate in the spring.

There was one last thing he wanted to mention—a name change, not from Ellis & Daughter to something like Ellis & Son. No, Sabrina was still involved in the business. He'd rolled through several options. Ellis Design Co., Ellis Restorations...he just hadn't narrowed it down to one yet.

He thankfully wrapped up the last strand of lights just as the choir started up with their rendition of *O Holy Night*.

He headed for the rear of the chapel. There, he left the Christmas lights twinkling in shades of white and gold, giving the chapel an almost magical look.

He laughed to himself. He was becoming as bad as Sabrina. They were just lights.

He gathered his supplies and quietly slipped out of the chapel. He made his way to the lodge, intending to ask Brandon and Sabrina if there was a way to auto-tune the choir or if they had a backup plan.

Maybe the guests would be too drunk to find the choir anything but hilarious.

He dropped his tools off in a utility closet off the back door and sought out his sister. As he looked around the space, he swelled with pride. Guests happily moved around the lodge in groups. Some sat in front of the Christmas tree. Others were engaged in a Christmas cookie decorating contest in the restaurant. He made his rounds to ensure the evening was moving forward without a hitch. The last thing he wanted was for unhappy guests so close to Christmas.

Two weeks ago, he would've worked himself up before he approached strangers, introvert overthinker that he was. Now, he swept in and out of conversations easily.

No one judged him as hard as he judged himself. And he was getting better at being kinder to himself.

After his rounds, he found Brandon and Sabrina standing together behind the reception desk.

They wore concerned looks.

"Why the long faces? Did you guys hear the choir? They're not that bad."

When neither laughed at his lame attempt at a joke, an odd feeling settled over him. "What's wrong?"

Sabrina and Brandon exchanged a look before Brandon gestured for him to follow them to the staff-only corridor.

"You guys are freaking me out. What's going on?"

Sabrina worried her hands over one another. "It's Emma. She's gone."

Chapter Twenty-Five

"What do you mean, gone? She couldn't exactly leg it out of here. We're nearly an hour from anywhere."

Brandon rubbed the skin between his eyes. "I saw her hop into the back of a car. It had one of those ride-share service stickers on the back. She had all her things. She returned the key in the drop box by the front desk."

A feeling of dread settled down on Caleb. Words were unreachable to him at that moment.

"She left a note in her cabin, addressed to you." Brandon handed it to him. Emma's signature handwriting was missing—just a quick scrawl of his name littered the front.

Caleb's heart raced as he tore open the envelope. What could it possibly contain that could explain her sudden disappearance?

He tugged the card out and read.

Caleb,
I think I got caught up in the Christmas magic of this place. I never meant to hurt you. But it's time for me to

return to the real world. I'm sorry. I knew you would try to talk me out of it, so I took the coward's way out.

Please forgive me.

Emma

He shoved the card unceremoniously back into the envelope. "Apparently, we all live in a dream world."

Sabrina and Brandon exchanged another glance. "I don't think that's quite the reason she left. I have it on good authority that that ex of hers was nosing about."

Oh. Well, that made sense, then. He couldn't blame her. He was rich and good-looking. Davis could offer her a life Caleb never could.

God, he was so good at hurting his feelings. Why had he let himself fall so quickly? He felt like the biggest idiot in the Commonwealth right about now.

"They didn't leave together, if that's what you're wondering. He huffed off a couple of hours before she left," Brandon said. "And the biddies —"

"Does it matter?" He shook off his feelings. Emma owed him nothing. She'd been honest with him from the very start. *So why do I feel like throwing up?*

Maybe she was right. They were living in a dream world. The bubble would've popped eventually.

"I think it matters very much," Brandon said. "Considering that I think she's running scared."

The last thing he wanted was to continue this conversation. "I'm going to my room for the night, unless I'm needed elsewhere?"

Sabrina frowned. "But there's the concert and drinks afterward."

"I've heard enough of the choir already. I'll see you guys tomorrow."

"Tomorrow is Christmas Eve," Sabrina called after him. "Don't think you can hide out in your room all day!"

He made a vague gesture to show he'd heard her, then slipped down the stairwell toward the second floor.

All he wanted was to be alone. None of this would be happening if his family had just left him alone in the first place.

He slammed his key card against the reader by his door and fell into bed, still fully clothed. If life were merciful, maybe he could find a way to sleep through Christmas.

* * * *

If her driver didn't shut the hell up, she was going to lose her mind well before they reached DC.

First, Marge had rattled on about her most recent divorce—she was hoping to find husband number six in the new year. Now, she was trying to convince Emma to sign up for her multi-level marketing scheme. *That totally isn't a scam, no siree, Bob.*

Thankfully, her phone began to ring as they hit the endless traffic that started roughly an hour outside of DC. She didn't have much faith that Marge knew her way into the city, so she was taking her as far as Alexandria. Emma would catch the metro from there.

Emma would've preferred a conversation with a telemarketer over being told the wonders of 'sparkling candles with money inside' for one more second.

Luckily, it was Aniyah on the other end.

"Hey," Emma said. "Why are you calling me tonight? Aren't you busy?"

Marge met her eyes in the rearview mirror and let out a little huff at the interruption.

"I got a notification that your location changed. Why are you no longer at Sky House?"

Emma winced her eyes shut. Why had she forgotten to remove location tracking? She and Aniyah had always kept tabs on each other, going back to their time in foster care. She didn't think Aniyah checked it much these days—after all, she had her own family to look after.

Clearly, she was wrong.

"I had to get back to the city," was the lame excuse Emma came up with.

Aniyah's sigh crackled along the line. "What happened?"

Marge turned on the traffic report at full volume. Emma covered her phone. "Can you turn that down a little, please, Marge? My sister is on the phone."

Marge harumphed to that but did as asked. Emma leaned back into her seat. "I think I was living in delulu land."

She could picture Aniyah on the other end of the phone, her index finger massaging the spot between her eyes. "You are too practical for delusion, Emma. You were developing business plans the last time we spoke. So, what happened? I've got all night."

"No, you don't." She knew that Aniyah was probably on her way out the door for a holiday event. She'd healed her childhood trauma by being a fantastic mother. Those kids were so lucky to have a mom who packed as much magic as possible into the holidays.

"So, beloved, please get to the point. What happened?" Aniyah said.

"Fine. Davis showed up."

"What? You left Mr. Lumberjack Dreamboat to go back to DC with *Davis?* Put that pale-eyed menace on the phone right now. Better yet, put me on speakerphone."

"I'm not with him. He came in like a tornado and left me like the remnants."

Aniyah sighed. "Setting aside the insensitive analogy, I get where you're coming from. So, what happened?"

Aniyah interrupted roughly every two words as Emma explained Davis' payment plan to her.

"Are you fucking kidding me? That little weasel can't get you back, so he wants to bankrupt you instead. Oh my god, I'm going to kick his ass. Better yet, I'm going to send my cousins to kick his ass. It'll only take them an hour or so to get there from PG county."

"We both know he would stroke out if he ever saw them, so please don't. I'm just going back to the condo to pack up my things and figure out where I'm going next."

"And Davis will be there too, presumably?"

"No. I texted him after he left to let him know I was going back to the city and would leave a check for him. He told me he'd be out of state until after the New Year, so I could stay there if I wanted to. So at least I'll have the place to myself."

"So, you're really giving him money? Seriously? He has no leg to stand on."

If anyone could understand the worry and anxiety bubbling up in her throat, it would be Aniyah. Growing up with an uncertain future meant she'd never allowed herself to get too comfortable. Paying Davis his discounted rate now meant that she could be done with him and still have a decent amount of savings to live off while she figured things out.

"We both know how petty he can be. I'd rather pay him half and be done with it. I'm already looking at an Airbnb to stay at while I apply for jobs. I'll be okay for a few months, especially if I receive unemployment benefits when my severance ends. Those checks will start coming in the new year."

"Wait, what about the stationery store? Aren't you going back to Falling Leaves? That sounds like the perfect next step for you, Em."

When Emma said nothing, Aniyah only sighed once more. "Don't tell me you left without saying goodbye."

"I left a note. I can't go back there. It was some sort of Christmas-induced hallucination. They need me in the real world."

"Falling Leaves *is* in the real world. You could have a home there if you wanted."

Emma's gaze moved to the haze of red brake lights ahead of them. "No. It's better to start over. It's too late to look back."

There was a ruckus in the background as Aniyah corralled her kids toward the car. "You just left like two hours ago. There's still time."

Emma had had enough of this conversation. She'd rather talk to Marge about her sparkly money candles.

"I've gotta go, Aniyah. I'll talk to you tomorrow, okay?"

She ended the call to Aniyah's protests. Then she promptly put her phone in do-not-disturb mode.

All she needed was a good night's sleep. Then she'd figure out the rest.

Chapter Twenty-Six

It turned out that when no one was around, Davis was a slob.

Wet towels were piled on the bedroom floor. His bed was unmade, with the sheets kicked and twisted around as if he'd performed gymnastics in his sleep. Even his thousand-dollar suit was crumpled on the floor.

This was evidence that he'd really seen her more as a live-in assistant with bedroom privileges than a true partner.

As Emma looked around, she wondered if she'd really known Davis at all. How many times had he bitched at her for leaving little piles in her wake? Meanwhile, he'd left an empty sushi container on the nightstand that had started to stink.

He must've had the cleaners coming a lot more frequently than he'd said. No wonder he had a lengthy list of charges for her. She was surprised he hadn't had them sweep in before she arrived. Given the upcoming holiday, he'd probably refused to pay their higher rates.

Leaving yet another mess for her. She debated deducting a cleaning fee from the monies owed. How had he made such a mess in a little over a week?

Knowing that he had cameras in the main areas of the condo, she sent him a text.

You left this place a pigsty. I'll clean up before I leave, but that cleaning fee will be paid out of the money I owe.

Almost immediately, three little dots appeared. She nervously gnawed on her lip. If Davis told her she had to leave, she'd have to use even more of her savings to find a hotel. Thankfully, although her ex-fiancé was a bastard, there was still a shriveled heart buried deep inside his chest.

Okay, that's fine. I've pretty much packed up most of what I'm taking, anyhow. I'll be selling most of the furniture. I'll be back on New Year's Eve – you can leave the check on my desk. You can deduct $500 for cleaning the place up before you leave. Sorry, I left in a hurry.

They both knew he was lying on both counts – this mess had taken days to accumulate, and that he had any regrets forcing her to pay him back.

But he wasn't worth the energy to argue with. She replied to his message with a thumbs-up and began cleaning.

She turned off all the big lights in the apartment and flicked on lamps in every room. Then, she turned the TV on to one of those Christmas atmosphere videos, with jolly music and a cheerful holiday scene in the background.

That only made her remember leaving Sky House, and Caleb. So, she switched to a true crime video instead.

The first thing she did was strip the bed and start a load of laundry. She couldn't sleep on the same sheets he had — that seemed too weird now.

By the end of the year, which was literally next week, she'd have no place to live and her income would be a third of what it once was. That wouldn't even cover rent, let alone other expenses of living in one of the most expensive cities in the country.

She couldn't help but compare this feeling of dread to the dread that would accompany an unfamiliar car in her foster family's driveway. It was almost always her social worker whisking her off to another placement. She'd always wonder what she'd done wrong. But the answer was usually nothing. The foster parents had grown tired of caring for children, especially when they realized the money they got from the state didn't match up with the hassle of trying to raise kids who had been through more in their short lives than most people went through in decades.

As she snapped the fitted sheets on the bed, she exhaled. She'd managed before, and she'd do it again. At the end of the day, she had to remember that she was on her own. She couldn't rely on anyone but herself. She'd made the mistake in trusting Davis. She should be grateful that she was saved from making the same mistake with Caleb.

Once she'd cleaned up the bedroom and taken two bags of stinky trash to the chute, she collapsed into bed.

* * * *

"Caleb, wake up."

Was he experiencing déjà vu, with his sister waking him up again out of a dreamless, depressed nap?

"I don't want to, and you can't make me," he mumbled into the pillow.

"You have a phone call. It came through on the front desk phone."

"Is it about Olivia and the girls?"

He rolled over and opened his eyes, wincing against the sunlight streaming through the faded curtains.

"Don't you think I asked that? It's not. But it's still important."

"What time is it?"

"A little after eleven." She shoved the cordless phone at him and closed the door.

He cleared his throat to dislodge his tongue from the roof of his mouth. He'd clearly been asleep far too long.

"Hello?"

"Is this Caleb Ellis?"

"Yes, it is. Who am I speaking to?"

"Caleb." The woman exhaled a large breath. "My name is Aniyah Goode. I'm Emma's foster sister."

An odd sensation settled in his stomach. "She's mentioned you before. What can I do for you?"

"I'm assuming by now you read her note and realized she skipped town as if she'd just passed a bunch of bad checks."

He had to laugh at the analogy. "Yes, unfortunately."

"Look, I know she'll probably kill me for contacting you. She'll say I overstepped her boundaries or something. But I've known Emma since we were teenagers. Going on a decade and a half now. I'd like to think I know her better than anybody. And I know she's running scared."

As much as he appreciated Aniyah wanting to have her best friend's back, he was still a little salty that he'd been left with nothing more than a Dear John letter.

"Back into the arms of her asshole ex? I've heard he was poking around here yesterday."

"Yes, he was. First to win her back. When that didn't work, he provided her with a bill for everything he's covered while they were together. His salary was triple hers. He'd insisted they'd live together in his fancy Capitol Hill condo. She contributed both financially and emotionally. But now Davis is saying he'll sue her for damages if she doesn't pay up."

Rage simmered deep in his stomach. "That sounds absurd. Does he even have a case?"

"He can take her to small claims court. Will he win? Probably not. He could draw it out, and make her miserable in the process. But he's offering her a discounted rate if she pays off the amount before the new year."

He dropped his elbows to his knees. "And how much is that?"

"Five thousand dollars. Emma has always been anxious about money. So that's why she rushed back. Not to be with Davis."

"We could've helped her if she'd let us."

Aniyah sighed. "Emma *also* has a terrible time asking for help. I'd blame her upbringing, but I think it goes deeper than that. She's also a Taurus."

He laughed, despite himself. "So am I."

"Oh, lord help us all. Well, Emma's feeling ashamed, and I think that's why she ran. Like she doesn't deserve any happiness."

"That's bullshit. She deserves happiness. She could be happy here if she'd let herself."

"So, you're not mad that she ran?"

He sat up and rubbed his hand through his hair. "Of course not. I was sad, sure. But I wasn't even mad when I thought she ditched me for her ex. I figured things had come to an end. But now...I want to help her. Whether she'll accept my help or not, I don't know. But I want to try."

Aniyah let out a chuckle. "I was hoping you'd say that. Look, I have an idea. It's a little crazy, being that it's Christmas Eve and all, but I think it just might work."

Fuck it. If Emma truly wanted to go her own way, he'd let her. But he had to try. He'd lain in bed half the night trying to figure out some sort of plan to get through to her. Aniyah tracking him down to help had to be some sign.

Caleb shot to his feet. "Okay, hit me with it."

"Do you have a pen? You're going to need to write some of these instructions down."

After fumbling around his room for a pen and locating a Sky House notepad, he returned to his place on the bed. "I'm ready."

Chapter Twenty-Seven

DC was one of those cities that emptied out around the holidays. It seemed nearly everyone Emma knew was from somewhere else. Even her. She'd grown up in the DMV — DC, Maryland and Virginia — but she'd hardly ever come into the city until she was a teenager. Except for field trips or the odd trips with her grandmother when they had a little extra cash.

Despite her not having a biological family, she'd never spent the holidays alone. Before Davis, she'd flown to Texas to spend the holidays with Aniyah and her family. Still, she'd always had that hollow place where she missed the feeling of family she'd never had.

She decided to embrace her aloneness. On Christmas Eve morning, she left the apartment early for breakfast. A few flakes of snow drifted past her on her way to her local coffee shop.

An odd sort of melancholy tugged at her as she walked. No matter what, nothing about this neighborhood would be local to her after next week.

She'd always felt a little out of place here, even after she'd committed to marrying into this life with Davis.

She looked down at her empty ring finger. Funny how she hadn't really noticed its absence while she was at Sky House.

She didn't really miss it now. Perhaps the certainty that came with living with Davis. Even though he'd told her she wouldn't have to work when they'd moved to New York, she never would've taken him up on that offer. Her gut instincts would've never let her fully depend on anyone but herself.

Obviously, her gut instinct had been right about that. She could only imagine the shenanigans he'd have pulled if she'd moved to New York and changed her mind before he'd gotten her down the aisle.

She hunkered down in the corner of the café with her coffee and croissant. Instrumental Christmas music played in the background. Several staff members wore Santa hats. She felt a pang of longing for the Christmas she'd given up when she fled Sky House.

She'd taken the coward's way out. She knew that. But wasn't it best that way? Caleb probably would've tried to come up with a plan to help her out. Or, god forbid, loan her money or something. That wouldn't solve the issue — making her beholden to him. That was exactly what she was hoping to avoid.

She brushed off those thoughts and began working on her résumé, sending requests for references to colleagues and old bosses, updating her career-focused social media, and scouring for jobs. With it being the holidays, she didn't expect to hear much until January. But she felt better knowing those emails were on their way.

The job market was discouraging. She'd been at her last job for nearly five years. It seemed as if the job search had changed almost completely since then. Jobs paid less but wanted you to do even more for your wage.

She reached into her bag, pulling out a brightly colored to-do list notepad. She added the following to her list—

Search for a recruiter??
Look into Master's degree programs??
Work in a stationery shop?

The first two options failed to enthuse her, and the third wouldn't pay the bills. But having options was the way forward. By the time she left the café, it was mid-afternoon. Not in a huge hurry to return to Davis' cold condo, she decided to stop at the grocery store to get the ingredients for a holiday dinner.

Just because she was alone that didn't mean that she couldn't be festive. Besides, she was used to making the best out of a bad situation by now.

* * * *

"I can't believe we're doing this."

After he'd ended the phone call with Aniyah, Caleb had swept into action. He wasn't in his right mind. That's why he'd asked his mom for help with his plan.

It wasn't his fault. She was standing at the front desk and noticed him "whirling around like one of those Turkish dancers," in her words. Somehow, that had turned into Lainey roping in the rest of the biddies. Babs, Inez, Tiffany, Tinesha, and the newest and most reluctant biddie, Sabrina's former roommate, Eleanor, were all in favor of ditching their families on Christmas Eve to help with his hair-brained plan.

Well, to be fair, it was *Aniyah's* plan. He was just following it. He had no idea if Emma would embrace him or slam the door in his face.

Aniyah knew Emma better than anyone. She was sure it was the former. But even if it was the latter, he could say that he tried. He'd never force someone to be with him. She was running scared, thanks to Davis' threat. He hoped she'd see that they were in this together. Whatever help she needed, he'd be there to support her.

So now, he was circling Emma's block, desperately looking for street parking that would fit the van, trying to ignore their bickering behind him.

"Aniyah says there's a garage around the corner. Just park there. You're never going to find street parking at this time of day, not even on a holiday," Inez said.

"Yeah, and it's probably forty bucks an hour," Caleb muttered to himself.

"Now is not the time to be miserly, Caleb," Babs cut in.

He turned to his mother in the passenger's seat. "I still don't know how all of you didn't have plans tonight."

"Look, Christmas is every year. There will never be another opportunity for us to see you make a romantic gesture like this," Lainey replied.

"Or see me make an idiot out of myself." He flicked on the turn signal as they approached the parking garage. "I swear to god, if I see any of you with your phones out, or god forbid, start *going live* when we see Emma, I will flip my shit."

"Language," Lainey chided.

"Don't worry, we'll keep them in check," Eleanor said. She pointed to Tiffany and Tinesha.

Inez clucked her tongue against her teeth. "You're no damn fun. Fine. My phone will stay in my bag. Happy?"

Caleb rolled down the window and took the ticket as they entered the parking garage. "Not really, but I'll take it."

After they parked, it was an ordeal to get all the biddies out of the van and organized. He wondered if herding cats would be easier.

"Okay, Aniyah gave me the address. I have a walking map up on my phone," Tinesha said.

"Why does she get to have her phone out and I don't?" Inez said.

"Because I have self-control." Tinesha gave Inez a light punch on the shoulder.

Caleb snickered. "Come on, it's starting to get dark. Aniyah said Emma just got home. Let's go get her."

* * * *

Considering she'd pulled everything together so last minute, she was quite pleased with her cozy Christmas Eve.

She'd cobbled together a decent Christmas dinner for one from ready meals available at the grocery store. This included her childhood favorite—a fruit cake. Something Davis had always forbidden at their celebrations. She was always the only one who ever loved them. She was sure there was a metaphor in there about feeling unwanted — growing up in foster care, and how everyone hated fruit cake — but she was depressed enough. She didn't need to make herself feel worse.

She turned on a cozy, atmospheric Christmas video to add to the ambience. Unlike last night, it didn't make her want to cry. That was something, right? She was starting to accept that her time at Sky House had been nothing more than a fantasy.

During her packing, she'd found a box of Christmas decorations. She'd never bothered to decorate much. Davis detested clutter, and they were usually away for the holidays anyway.

She'd looked over the campy decorations that had been hidden in a box for years. Her pink desktop Christmas tree went on the coffee table. The bold, retro table runner laid across on the glass and metal dining table.

Brightly colored pillows were tossed on the leather couch. She even found her old, tattered Rudolph doll from childhood.

She sat on the couch, clutching the old doll. Even after finally allowing her personality to shine in this cold place, it still felt like someone else's home.

It was time to make her own home now, for better or worse. She couldn't rely on anyone else.

She'd relied too heavily on Davis. Look where that had left her.

The microwave beeped, reminding her that her dinner for one was done reheating.

She gently placed Rudolph on the couch and headed for the kitchen. Her holiday spirit dipped slightly when she pulled out the plate of turkey, stuffing and mashed potatoes.

"At least you have a meal," she muttered to herself. "It could be worse."

She closed the microwave door and set her plate on the table. She remembered she'd bought gravy. That would save the turkey that looked about as dry as Davis' sense of humor.

She began to rifle through her grocery bags as the jarring noise of the doorbell cut through the apartment. Her heart jumped into her throat at the interruption.

Most of the building was empty, but someone must've rung her bell by mistake. Better send them on their way.

She shook out her nerves as she walked over to the door. She unlatched the deadbolt and opened the door wide enough for the chain latch to catch.

"Sorry, wrong apartment! Merry Christmas!"

When she started to close the door, a hand caught it before it could catch. "Emma, please open the door."

Chapter Twenty-Eight

Emma peered at him through the crack in the door. Through the narrow space, he couldn't read her expression, and he hated that.

Thank god he'd insisted the biddies stay downstairs. They were probably driving the security guy crazy by now. But he didn't need to see the whole of her face to know she was more than a little freaked out.

She blinked once, then twice, before she spoke. "How did you know where I was?"

"Aniyah told me. This was her idea." He released his hand from the door. It was promptly pushed shut. Muffled Christmas music filtered out from under the door. He caught his reflection in the glossy surface. Perhaps this was for the best. He'd tried. She wasn't receptive. He stood there, rapidly losing hope, before the door unlatched and came fully open.

"Well, you came all this way. You should come in." She stepped to the side. They brushed against one another as he passed into the apartment.

He cast a quick look around as Emma came behind him to close the door. This place was as sterile as a doctor's office. Save the random bits of colorful Christmas decorations thrown around. Even the Christmas music she was playing was quirky, a playlist titled *Vintage Weirdo Christmas*.

That was all Emma. She was a maximalist stuck in a minimalist's world. He hated that she'd been stifled for so long. Even if he never saw her again after tonight, he wanted the best for her.

"Davis isn't here, right?"

She locked the door behind them. "No. He's in Vail, Aspen, or one of those hoity-toity ski resorts in Colorado. I didn't care enough to ask for clarification."

She stood by the door, arms folded. Somehow, she was still slightly intimidating, even given her pajamas dotted with quotes from *National Lampoon's Christmas Vacation*.

"I guess I won't pussyfoot around things. Aniyah told me what happened with Davis, how he's asking you for money. That's why you left, isn't it?"

She rubbed her hands along her forearms as if she'd caught a chill just by talking about the man.

"He told me he'd reduce the amount I owed if I paid him by the end of the year. He's letting me stay here while I figure things out. I'll pay him before I go."

It broke his heart that she had given up so easily. But he understood the shame she must be feeling. The need to fix the problem on her own, because asking for help was too overwhelming.

"Jeez, what a generous guy. Someone should carve his likeness out of marble or something."

When Emma said nothing, he carried on. "I could've helped you, Emma. Firstly, by telling you that dickhead

Davis can itemize every expense that he wants. It doesn't mean you owe him anything. Unless you had a written agreement?"

She brushed past him on the way to the kitchen. "We didn't. But I just want to be done with him. I know he'll probably try to sue me just for shits and giggles. He'll draw this out for months, just to torture me."

He watched as she opened the microwave, frowned, and closed it again. "No gravy in the world is gonna save that sad display," she said.

"You still don't have to pay him, Emma. You have options. I could've helped. Aniyah said —"

"I never should've told her anything. I knew she'd get involved somehow. I just didn't think like this. She should become an honorary member of the biddies."

He let out a nervous laugh. "Yeah, about them. They're all downstairs."

Her eyes boggled. "You brought them with you?"

He shrugged. "It was my mom's idea. Once they get an idea in their heads, it's kind of impossible to stop it."

She shook her head. "Look, Caleb. I appreciate you coming up here on Christmas Eve, of all days. But I think we both got caught up in a fantasy world. Being back in the city has brought me back to reality."

She wouldn't meet his eyes. It was as if she knew what she was saying wasn't true.

"If you're saying Falling Leaves is a fantasy world, you clearly haven't spent enough time there."

She cracked a smile at that. "You know what I mean. I guess I should be thankful to Davis, in a way. He brought me back to earth. Made me realize I can't rely on anyone but myself."

"By attempting to extort you when you wouldn't get back with him? Come on, Emma. We both know that's all bullshit. You could have something in Falling Leaves. Even if it's not with me, your business idea is fantastic. You'd have the whole town's support."

He wanted to bring her into his arms. To comfort her, to show her that she was no longer alone.

Neither of them had to do things on their own anymore. They just had to be brave enough to lean on one another.

She shook her head sadly. "Look what happened the last time I thought I could depend on someone. He's threatening to sue me. I just..." She turned away from him. "I can't take that risk again. I'm terrified. I'd rather rely on myself than anyone else."

He said nothing. He couldn't imagine the betrayal and fear she must be feeling now. There was no gentle platitude he could say to convince her.

He had to show her.

He walked around so he was facing her. She wiped at her face. There was no mistaking the tears staining her cheeks. She looked up at him. "You should go. If you leave now, you can maybe make the tail end of your family celebrations."

His phone dinged with a series of texts. "I'm not missing anything." He showed her his phone. "Everyone is invested in this...in *you*, Emma. We've only known you a couple of weeks, but that's long enough to know we love you."

Her mouth parted. "Love? Like...for real? That just doesn't seem possible."

Maybe his mouth told a truth his heart wasn't quite ready to hear. But he didn't regret his words. "I've never felt like this before, Emma. I'm not the type to make bold declarations like this. You can ask the biddies if you want. They're probably on their way up here, anyway."

She let out a noise that was halfway between a laugh and a cry. "You really mean it, don't you? You want me to stay, even if things didn't work out between us? I'd be right next door, Caleb."

He took a step toward her, his hands coming to her face. "I'm not saying it would be easy. But you deserve this chance, Emma. And I'm not so selfish that I wouldn't want you to have it if things didn't work out between us."

The thing was, he had that feeling in his gut that told him Emma was it. He could see a life with her by his side, sprawling out ahead of him.

But he couldn't, no, *wouldn't* force her to do anything she didn't want to.

She rested her head against his hand. "It just seems too easy. When Davis showed up, it brought me back to reality. Reminded me that I didn't deserve to have this kind of dream come true."

"Fuck Davis," Caleb said. "You deserve this, Emma. You deserve the whole world."

Their eyes met. She placed her hand on top of his. "So, you'll have me? Even though I'm a mess?"

"It'll be our mess, then. I meant what I said, Emma. I love you. I'm here if you want me to be. The rest will come later. The business, our relationship, melding our families… This is the hardest part, Em. Once you say yes, I have a sneaking suspicion everything else is going to fall into place."

She closed her eyes, keeping her hand on top of his. Caleb's heart thrummed in his chest. It hadn't been more than a few seconds since he'd stopped speaking.

It felt like years. Like time had slowed down, because she was with him.

She was home.

After a long moment, her eyes reopened. "I'm in it if you are."

Before she could utter another breath, he swept her into his arms. Their mouths found each other just as the doorbell began to ring.

They broke apart, laughing. "I swear, they've got to be psychic or something."

"I guess if I'm choosing you, the biddies are part of the deal?"

He rolled his eyes. "I promise they leave me alone most of the time."

She stole another kiss. "Better let them in, then, huh?"

He held her close for just another moment. "In a minute."

As they stood intertwined, Caleb had never been surer about anything in his life. This woman was his future.

Chapter Twenty-Nine

Once the biddies made their way inside, a chaotic whirl of Christmas cheer took over Davis' apartment.

Oh, Emma could only imagine how his shriveled, Grinch-like heart would hate the laughter and joy filling his sterile space. She chuckled to herself, picturing him sniffing the air dramatically once he returned from his trip. He would drive himself insane trying to recognize the smells, and then he'd bathe the place in bleach. If he even knew where to find it.

Of course, somehow, they'd managed to bring an entire turkey dinner along with them. Inez, Lainey, and Eleanor kept busy in the kitchen while the rest of the biddies began to tackle the packing with Emma and Caleb.

It all felt right, except for the little issue about Davis' requested payment. But, of course, they'd thought of that, too.

"Look, if you want just to be done, you can pay him a fuck-you payment if you want. I suggest going to the bank and paying it all in pennies. Then, leave the wheelbarrow in front of the door on the way out so he has to crawl over it on his way back inside. But I've been known to be petty," Eleanor said.

"You don't have to pay him a dime," Inez called from the kitchen. "Let him sue you! We'll take care of him. Rich boys like that need to learn they can't push people around. You're not alone, Emma. We're your backup."

She looked worriedly at Caleb, who placed a hand on her shoulder. "You need that money for the store, don't you?"

She nodded. "Yeah. He doesn't know about that. He just wanted to find a way to punish me, I guess."

"You know, Mayor Ford is a practicing attorney," Tinesha said. "I bet I could get him to draft up a good 'screw you' letter to leave your smarmy ex."

She collapsed onto the couch. "How do you have an answer for everything?"

"We had a lot of time to think on the drive up here," Babs deadpanned. "Now come on, let's eat this Christmas dinner. We've got a long night ahead of ourselves."

As they gathered at the table, pushing in chairs and sitting on upturned boxes, Emma took a moment to be grateful. She'd almost thrown all of this away.

And for what? Because she'd been scared? She was smart enough to know that the trauma that was built into your bones didn't vanish overnight. She'd run, but because she'd always wanted to stay ahead of the trouble life had thrown her way.

Caleb grabbed her knee under the table. "You doing okay, Em? I know this is a lot."

She set her fork down and placed her hand on top of his. "I'm sorry I ran off, Caleb. I won't do that again, I promise. Add another thing onto my to-do list after the move — finding a new therapist." She eyed the biddies. "Don't tell me one of you is a practicing therapist on top of everything else?"

Lainey laughed. "No, but we do know the best one in town. We can get you to the top of the waiting list. I know we may seem like a bunch of country bumpkins sometimes, but we've all been on our own healing journeys, you know?"

"Once you've survived menopause, everything else is a breeze," Babs said.

The table erupted into laughter, and everyone broke into separate conversations once more.

Caleb exhaled and rubbed his thumb over her knee. "I'm not going to say that it didn't devastate me when you left. I felt like I was back where I started, before Sabrina and Brandon forced me to work at Sky House. Depressed and alone."

"I'm sorry I made you feel that way, Caleb."

He squeezed her knee, as his jaw worked, as if he was working out what to say. She gazed at him, slightly distracted by the golden twinkle in his eyes, before he began to speak again. "But once Aniyah called me, the pieces came into place. I understood why you did it. You and I have a lot of things in common, but one is that we're both terrible at asking for help."

"Well, we *were*. I know I've got more folks behind me who will go to bat for me. Good thing, because I think Aniyah is getting tired of handling that duty all by herself."

Emma's phone began to buzz across the tabletop. "Speaking of." She squeezed his hand before answering the video call.

"Well, it's about goddamned time," Aniyah deadpanned. "Not one of you could've called me to give me an update? I've been waiting on pins and needles over here!"

Emma tilted the phone around the table, allowing Aniyah to get a look at everyone. "Sorry, we got a little busy," Inez said. "But you knew it went well, didn't you? We don't do things halfway."

Aniyah laughed. "I haven't even met you and I already know that. My girl is in good hands with y'all."

Emma turned the phone toward her so she could see her best friend, her sister, if not by blood then by heart. She was waving her hand in front of her face. "Y'all are gonna make me mess up my makeup before church."

"I love you, Aniyah. Thank you for being an honorary biddie and helping me see what I was about to miss out on," Emma said.

Aniyah's face crumpled like a tissue. "Okay, okay. I've gotta go before I really mess up my face. I love you too, Em. Merry Christmas."

By the time they started loading the van, it was well after midnight. She realized just how little of her life remained in this place—no more than twenty boxes loaded onto dollies and out of the apartment.

In the brief moment she was alone before Caleb and the biddies came back to gather her and the remaining boxes, she stepped into Davis' office. She opened the top drawer of his desk and pulled out a blank sheet of his personal letterheaded paper.

She took a moment to admire it—she'd picked out the fine 28 lb paper and designed his personal branding.

She slammed it down on the tabletop and reached for his fountain pen.

D –

Every trace of me is gone now. If you find anything I missed, you can toss it. As for what I 'owe' you, please forward any requests to the Falling Leaves, Virginia town hall, attention to Mayor Gary Ford, Esq. I've forwarded him a copy of your claims. He'll be looking them over after the holidays. I think we both know you might not have much luck with your suit, but if you want to pursue it, then don't hesitate to get in touch with Mr. Ford.

Thank you for showing me what I really want. Good luck in New York.

E

There was a fifty-fifty chance Davis would let it go. But either way, she wouldn't be bullied into submission, not anymore.

She placed the letter atop his keyboard as Caleb appeared in the doorway. "You ready to go?"

She dropped the fountain pen back into the drawer and closed it. "Ready as I'll ever be."

Chapter Thirty

They arrived back at Sky House sometime after sunrise. Caleb and Emma walked in, hand-in-hand. Emma took a moment to pause at the front desk.

"It's hard to believe it was only a couple of weeks ago when I first saw you standing there. It feels like years."

He chuckled. "Is that a good thing or a bad thing?"

"A good thing. It feels like I've known you forever."

Caleb wrapped both arms around her. "When you know, you know, right?"

She rested her head against his chest. "Thank you again, Caleb."

"For what?"

"For not giving up on me. Even when I gave up on myself."

He exhaled and pulled her closer. "I think we both knew you'd find your way back here eventually. I'm glad it was sooner, rather than later."

Sabrina and Brandon appeared from around the corner, wearing matching ugly Christmas sweaters featuring a choir of cats proclaiming *Meowy Christmas.*

"There you two are. I figured you'd want a moment to yourselves after spending the last day with the biddies."

Caleb snorted at that. "Like you aren't in cahoots with them half the time."

She gave an impish shrug. "I mean, they do get things right sometimes."

"They're two for two now," Brandon added.

"So now maybe you'll all stop protesting and just listen to us from now on?" Lainey popped out from behind the big Christmas tree.

"Maybe when you stop spying on us," Sabrina countered. "I see you, Inez, you can come out."

Inez appeared from the other side of the tree.

"Fine, come on. It's time for breakfast, anyhow."

Over breakfast, plans were hashed out for where Emma would be living once her stay at Sky House ended on January first. She decided to take up Sabrina's offer to live in her guest suite in her beautiful home in town. It was the busy season at the lodge, so Sabrina wouldn't be home as much. In exchange for a reasonable rent, she would take care of her two cats, Sarah and Jareth, and perform general upkeep on the property.

She was grateful that Sabrina had offered this opportunity. As much as she wanted to move in with Caleb right away, it was too early for such a drastic step. After all, they had his children to consider. She had her first unofficial meeting with the girls when Caleb video-called them after breakfast. She stayed in the background, only popping in the frame to say hello at the insistence of Caleb's ex-wife, Olivia.

It still felt odd…knowing Caleb had a family of his own. All the more reason to take things at their own pace. After all, there was no rush. Still, a part of her loved the idea of having children in her life, aside from Aniyah's kids, who she only saw a few times a year. She tried not to get ahead of herself, but she loved the idea of getting to know the girls.

They retreated to her cabin after breakfast to spend some much-needed time together. Emma took a moment to take it in as they entered, remembering the feelings of doubt and dread she'd had when she'd fled this place.

Now, as she looked around, she felt only comfort. She'd made the right choice.

Caleb sat on the edge of the bed. "Hey."

She grinned. "Hey."

He pulled her back onto the bed. They lay intertwined, their clothes still cold from the snowy weather outside.

"I just want you to know that I've always got your back, Em. I know this isn't going to be easy, especially with the girls. Things happened fast at first, but we're not in any kind of rush now."

She brought her hands to his chest.

"I'm glad you said that. This has felt a little overwhelming. Even though it feels right. The only kids I've been around are Aniyah's, and she lives in Texas. I just don't want to be a weirdo, you know?"

He laughed. "The girls will probably like you if you're willing to be weird and get on their level. Emerson's in kindergarten. Poppy will be in preschool next year. So, it makes more sense if they stay where their routines are. But they're here on the weekends and sometimes for longer stretches. I visit them there, too. So, they are a big part of my life."

"And there's really no co-parenting drama or anything like that?"

"Olivia is my friend, first and foremost. More than anyone, she's been eager for me to find someone else. She doesn't want me to be lonely."

Emma sighed. "I don't know. Maybe it's my cynicism, but it seems too good to be true."

He wrapped his arms around her. "We still argue. The girls are actual humans who have meltdowns, flip out, and are general assholes sometimes. But that's real life, you know? It's not always shiny and perfect." He cleared his throat and raised his voice several octaves. "You're not my mom, Emma!" He laughed. "Just giving you a preview of your future sans rose-colored glasses. But we've got a while before all of that."

"I know that." She exhaled. "I just need to relax and let things happen. I don't know why I'm feeling so anxious. This is a good thing."

"Honestly, I'd be a little worried if you weren't feeling anxious right now. Your entire life has flipped upside down. There's a lot of uncertainty. But you can be sure of one thing, and that's I'm not going anywhere. We'll get through this together."

She yawned against her arm. "That's the one thing I'm not worried about."

Caleb kissed the top of her head. "Well, good. Everything else is figure-out-able."

Emma curled herself around Caleb, feeling more comfortable than ever. She was asleep a moment later.

* * * *

Caleb and Emma likely would've slept through most of Christmas Day if the biddies hadn't intervened. The room was dark when the shrill noise of the cabin phone ringing woke them. Judging by the horrid jingling the phone emanated, it likely hadn't been used since the 1980s.

Emma cursed under her breath and rolled over. Caleb grabbed the phone and croaked out a greeting.

"Wake up, sleepyheads! We're having Christmas dinner at the house tonight. Be ready to go in an hour," Lainey said.

He groaned. "What time is it?"

"Nearly five. Your dad and uncle have been frying turkeys again, so the sooner we get home, the better the odds the house isn't engulfed in flames."

He covered the receiver and gave Emma a shake. "Are you okay going to my parents' house tonight?"

She let out a yawn. "Yeah, just give me a minute to take a shower, and I'll be good to go."

He uncovered the phone. "We'll be there."

Lainey laughed. "Well, of course you will be, sweetheart. See you soon."

* * * *

It didn't take much effort to get Emma out of the door. She kept talking about how this had been the first Christmas in years she'd been with family. Once the Ellis clan adopted you, there was no going back.

He had to park a block and a half away from his parents' house. They must've invited all the biddies and their families to boot.

As they approached the house, he tugged her closer. "I'd warn you about what you're walking into, but I think you know what to expect well enough by now."

The Ellis house was lit up with white Christmas lights, which clung to anything that stood still for long enough. As much as he'd wanted to run away from this place when he was younger, he knew now this was home.

"I kind of love the chaos. But if that ever changes, I'll let you know."

A dual yelp echoed throughout the night. He knew well enough to know it was his dad and uncle.

"Oh, jeez. I hope they're not burning the place down for real this time."

They rounded the corner to find Uncle Gordon pulling out what looked like a perfectly fried turkey.

"Well, I'll be damned. It worked this time!"

"If it didn't, I think your turkey fryer would find its way to the dump," Emma quipped.

Everyone laughed at that. "Come on, let's get this turkey inside. Everyone's hungry."

Once the turkey was safely inside, everyone made their way into the kitchen and dining room where the buffet was set up. He knew everyone in the room. Emma didn't yet, but she would soon.

"Look, Em." He pointed to the mantle. Nestled amongst the other stockings, there was a new one. It was made from a retro Christmas pattern. Totally Emma's style. Her name had been embroidered in a loopy, cursive font.

She reached over to admire it. "What? How?"

Sabrina appeared with a plate. "Oh, that's Mom's doing. She made one for Brandon before we were together, too. It's her superstition. That works, I guess. Welcome to the family, Em."

Caleb drew her in for a kiss. "Let's not scare her off just yet, huh? This is bad enough." He gestured around the room.

"I love it, though. I'm where I'm meant to be. I know that now."

"That makes two of us."

Epilogue

Fifteen months later

"A little to the left." Emma gestured to Caleb, who was awkwardly posed in the display window of Yours Truly, trying to get the angle just right on the sign in their spring display.

He nudged the sign to the right. "No, not my left, yours!"

Caleb cupped his hand to his ear. He mumbled something, not that she could hear him through the thick glass. This was her second spring in Falling Leaves, but the first since Yours Truly had been open.

The shop window just had to be perfect. But perfection was hard to come by if your husband couldn't hear you through the thick, hundred-year-old paned glass.

She swung open the bright yellow door and ducked her head inside. "A little to *your* left! It's almost there."

He nodded and nudged the hand-lettered sign a little to the left. Emma had spent weeks on it. Then, he paused to adjust the remaining display contents. Easter baskets brimming with different stationery supplies, soft, collectible rabbits, and other baby stuffed animals congregated in front of the display.

She clapped her hands together and rushed back inside for a final look.

"Perfect. Now, let's get up the bunting, and it's all done."

Caleb awkwardly ducked his head as he backed out of the window. He jumped from the stepladder. Once it was stowed away, he ran a hand down her bare arm. His golden wedding band caught the light. The whole husband-wife business was relatively new. They'd gotten married two weeks before Christmas—of course—in the chapel at Sky House. It seemed fitting that they'd had their wedding at the place where they'd first met.

And of course, she'd been a Christmas bride. Nothing else had made sense to her. The wedding had been a candlelight affair right at dusk. It'd started to snow as they took their vows.

"You've gone to the faraway place again, Em. You all right?" Caleb reached behind him for the pastel bunting. She'd made it herself during one of the shop's many craft nights.

"I was just thinking about our wedding. How perfect it was."

He set some of the bunting around her shoulders and tugged on it. She tumbled into his arms. "You really love me, don't you, kid?"

She rolled her eyes. "Not when you call me that, but sure, I do."

He brushed his knuckles against her chin. "Let's get this wrapped up. They're about to shut down the street for the celebration."

"Which one is it today? I swear, I thought fall was the big season for celebrations around here, but spring is giving it a run for its money," Emma said.

"The basketball finals parade, remember?"

Falling Leaves High had come in fourth at the All-State Basketball tournament back in February. They'd never so much as placed before. This was the kind of place where they didn't need an excuse to celebrate.

"All that fuss for fourth place," she joked. "But hey, it's not like I didn't sponsor one of the floats." After all, the motto she'd chosen for the business was *No occasion is too small to celebrate.* Her tiny little shop was the place everyone came to in town when there was a celebration or if they were looking for that special something. She'd curated the finest supplies of gifts, as well as invitations.

"At least you got Inez's pink truck towing your float and the Falling Leaves High cheerleaders. I think the Ellis & Co float is just a couple of the coaches pulled by a tractor."

She chuckled as she taped up the bunting. "I can't help that I run a business with a feminine motif, and yours is a construction business."

Ellis & Co would officially be Caleb's business after her father-in-law retired at the end of the year. Sabrina still helped with smaller projects, but Caleb now led their core crew.

Especially since baby girl Willow had made her debut last October. Sabrina had taken to motherhood like a duck to water. And now Emma had the title of aunt to the most perfect little girl in the world.

Well, aside from her stepdaughters.

Emerson and Poppy were well used to their Emmybear. Even she was surprised the nickname still hung around, given that Emerson was in second grade and Poppy was in kindergarten.

They locked up the shop and made their way to Silver Spring Street as the Falling Leaves High School band began to line up for the parade.

Somewhere in the crowd, a trumpet emitted a terrible noise. Caleb drew his arm around Emma. "Now, that's one thing that hasn't changed since I was in high school. The band isn't going to win any championships. There's a reason they pass out earplugs at football games."

Emma laughed. "Hey, it could be worse. They could be out there, I don't know...tipping cows or something."

It was such a beautiful spring morning. She couldn't imagine herself anywhere else. Not that she'd had much reason to leave town since moving here, except to go to the Lodge.

Davis hadn't taken too kindly to the letter she'd left in his condo, but his lawsuit had fizzled out before he could ever file it. Last she'd heard, he'd found a new girlfriend shortly after moving to New York.

Good riddance.

Other than a trip to see Aniyah and her family last summer, Falling Leaves felt too perfect to leave.

A crowd had already formed along Falling Leaves' main drag. Emma and Caleb slipped into the back. Not that they stayed hidden for long.

"Emma Ellis!" Her name came over a megaphone. "Get your little backside up on this truck!" Inez stood with the rest of the biddies in the back of her bright pink truck.

"You too, Caleb, come on! Your mom and dad are in the Ellis & Co float, there isn't any room for you."

They exchanged a glance. They'd both gotten better at not overthinking since they'd gotten together. She would've been mortified just a year ago to have all eyes on her.

Now, she grabbed Caleb's hand. "Come on, we both know they're not going to let up until we agree. Better to just go along with their schemes."

Caleb laughed. "They've taught you well."

They were both hoisted up in the back of the pink truck that Emma and the biddies had decorated with paper flowers. All of them were there, even the reluctant biddies like Eleanor and Tinesha.

"There's our best girl. Oh wait, we're missing one! Sabrina Blake! Get on up here!"

Sabrina made a half-hearted attempt to point at the baby strapped to her chest.

"That hasn't stopped you before," Babs said. "Besides, you're one of us, whether you want to admit it or not."

Sabrina rolled her eyes but made her way toward the truck with Brandon in tow.

"I hardly see how we're all going to fit up here," Brandon protested.

"The more, the merrier, and the less likely one of us will go winging out the back of the cab," Sabrina said.

Soon, they were all squeezed into the bed of the truck. Caleb brought his arm around the small of Emma's waist, drawing her close.

Somehow, she still felt butterflies nearly every time he touched her.

"I swear, it seems like half the damn town is in the parade." Sabrina pointed to the smattering of people waving from the sidewalk.

"Well, we've got to show off to somebody, even if it's to ourselves," Caleb said. "That's just the Falling Leaves way."

As the terrible marching band took up a god-awful rendition of Kendrick Lamar's *Not Like Us*, the parade was officially underway.

"Y'know, I thought about throwing pens or something at the crowd, then the mayor told me that could be a liability issue," Tinesha said.

"Ballpoint to the eye, not a great way to die," Brandon quipped.

Everyone laughed.

The band grew louder, and with everyone chattering, Emma stood back and took it all in. She couldn't imagine her life if she hadn't seen that fateful ad on social media all those months ago.

She'd found her forever in Falling Leaves.

Sign up for our newsletter and find out about all our romance book releases, eBook sales and promotions, sneak peeks and FREE romance books!

It Could've Been a Wonderful Life
Karin Baine

Excerpt

"No man is a failure who has friends."

Annie Marlowe's sneeze shot through her entire body as the parting words from Guardian Angel Clarence blazed across the screen.

"Pff-ft. What does that say about me, eh, George Bailey?" Annie asked her tufty-haired, toffee-coloured guinea pig named after her favourite movie character. He was the only one she had to talk to, and even that was a one-way conversation, since his defective squeak made him sound like a chewed dog toy.

He snuffled his little nose at the bars of his cage, looking for food, when he heard her opening the box of leftover pastries that Sam, her landlord, had brought her. There were some advantages to living above a coffee shop, even if moving there from her family home of over thirty years had felt like a step back at the time.

Fletchers Café was nestled on the corner of a row of shops that otherwise looked only fit for demolition. Faded advertising signs, cracked windows and graffiti-covered shutters told the story of the crisis-hit local economy. In contrast, the French-style bistro was an oasis of luxury for those busy office workers and people who wanted to catch up over a coffee that didn't come from a jar. Fletchers was a beacon of hope for future retail development and regeneration of the area.

Even Annie found some comfort there. The aroma of fresh bread and cakes baking in the oven reminded her of her mother, before that bastard cancer had got hold of her. Reliving those memories of her baking up a storm in the kitchen on a Sunday afternoon was as close as she could get to her mother now that she was gone forever.

Sam also kept her fed during the times she couldn't afford to go grocery shopping...*like now.*

"I should just paint a giant L for 'loser' on my forehead," she muttered as she took a bite of a *pain au chocolat.* The buttery layers melted with the chocolate filling on her tongue, every nibble dispensing a trail of flaky crumbs down her front.

George Bailey gave an asthmatic wheeze in agreement before giving a little popcorn kick and scooting sawdust over her bedroom floor. Annie didn't bother to sweep it up. There'd be a bigger pile to clean up by morning and it wasn't as though she was expecting any visitors.

She tossed another used tissue onto the growing collection littering the floor along with her clothes. The hard-worn beige carpet was almost completely covered with her mess, but it gave her a sense of ownership in a place she didn't yet think of as home. The magnolia décor was functional, but there was nothing exciting about it—kind of like her life at present. She needed to put her own stamp on the place. If she had the money or motivation, she'd redecorate—preferably with something far removed from her mother's predilection towards floral prints. Her festive spirit being in short supply this year, she hadn't even managed to put up her Christmas decorations.

Sitting there in her fleecy, gingerbread-man onesie, stuffing herself and bawling along to *It's a Wonderful Life*, she was the poster girl for loneliness.

She sneezed again and sprayed her pyjamas with a fine mist of chocolate saliva and crumbs. *Nice.*

"And you wonder why you can't keep a man? You're so classy." She yanked another tissue from the box on her nightstand. *Great.* Not only had she been dumped and was grieving for her mother, now she had a cold to contend with too.

Annie collapsed back onto the bed as tears threatened once more. She pulled the crocheted blue-and-pink blanket she'd kept from her mother's bed around her like a woolly cocoon. Her throat was burning with a sorrow she couldn't seem to shake off.

In a nutshell, her life was shit. Watching a film highlighting the value of friends and family when she had neither hadn't been the best idea, especially at a time when her mood was already dragging itself by the fingertips across the floor. It merely served as a reminder of how much she'd lost and how little she'd really accomplished with her own life.

Weary of the fight, she closed her eyes. With any luck, her blocked sinuses would suffocate her in her sleep and put her out of this misery.

* * * *

The December sky was so black that it was difficult to see the rain until the car headlights illuminated the kamikaze rain drops attempting to dodge discovery and soaking everything in their path.

"Don't you think you should slow down?" Flame flipped down the visor mirror on the passenger side of the Lamborghini and painted another coat of scarlet gloss across her lips.

David Reece cast a sideways glance at his date, who was now taking pouting selfies. It had been fun to date the darling of the tabloids for a minute, but there really wasn't anything behind that stage-managed façade. He didn't even know her real name, for goodness' sake. It was doubtful she did either, with her every move scripted for the cameras.

"We want to make an entrance, don't we? I thought that's what this was all about—grabbing headlines."

"Is that really all you think there is between us?" The concern he detected in her voice suggested that she might actually care about him. *Impossible.* No one did.

"Would it matter? I thought we were both only in this for the publicity? You get to pretend you've tamed the playboy millionaire and I get to boost my toy shop empire when customers believe they'll run into their idol shopping for stuffed animals." He wasn't in this charade of a relationship for anything else. Well, the sex had been good…when they'd had it.

"I need this, David."

The soft, unconfident voice sounded so unlike her. *Does she really think we're still in a relationship?* Since his divorce three years before, he hadn't been in the market for another long-term commitment. He was happy with his bachelor life. It was much less painful than being married to someone who'd loved his money more than him.

"Flame, this was only ever supposed to have been a bit of fun, and it was in the beginning, before we knew the press were interested. Now everything is a business transaction. There's no spontaneity, no intimacy anymore. We don't even see each other now, outside of these high-profile functions." These days, their simple want of each other's company had been traded for photo ops and press exposure. Suddenly it was no longer enough to keep him satisfied.

"Are you saying you want to end this?" She tightened her lips into a jammy red line as she primped her atomic red curls around her bare, perma-tanned shoulders. David couldn't help but wonder what she'd looked like pre-celebrity, before she'd succumbed to changing her appearance to suit society's version of beauty.

"I mean, I hadn't planned to—at least, not tonight—but yeah. It's been a fun ride, but I think it's run its course." Now the novelty of the relationship with Flame had worn off, like every other one he'd had since his divorce, and it was time to get out, especially if she was beginning to take it seriously.

"I thought we were both benefitting from this arrangement."

"We were, but we can't keep faking this forever. We'll meet other people…then things will get messy." Or worse, she'd expect some sort of commitment from him.

"I can't believe you're actually doing this when we're on our way to my movie premiere." Flame took several deep breaths, her pneumatic breasts rising perilously from the red velvet sweetheart line of her dress. One wrong move and there'd be a serious wardrobe malfunction hitting the front pages the next day. That would be an incident to devastate her, he was sure.

"There's no point in getting upset about it. I'm not going to do anything to spoil your big night."

"Except dump me."

"You can dump me, if you'd prefer. We can make a show of it. A public break-up would get you the headlines you want." The sympathy vote had worked in his favour when a cheating wife had brought record numbers of shoppers to his stores. Although, the reality of that particular betrayal had been painful at the time and too raw for him to enjoy the profits of his despair. He'd learned his lessons since then, though. These days he didn't let anyone get close enough to do that kind of damage again, and he appreciated the value of pre-nups. Now he made sure to take care of number one.

"You really don't know me at all, do you?"

"What do you mean?" David didn't have to turn his head to know those ice-blue eyes were trained on him, laden with disappointment.

"I'll bet you don't know anything about my career, never mind my personal circumstances."

"I know you did some reality dating show, and, er...had a pop career after that. To be fair, Flame, we never did go in for a lot of talking."

She sighed and gave him a wobbly smile. "I guess not. I want you to know I'm not just some fame-hungry wannabe. I don't care about any of that. This is just a job like any other to me. I'm simply waiting for that big payday so I can leave all this behind."

This was a brief glimpse of the real Flame. It was a shame she'd been hidden for so long. She was right. He didn't know the woman beside him at all.

"Then what?"

"I go back to my real life, as plain old Beverley Smith. By that time, I hope to have enough money to buy a place for me and my daughter."

David swerved the car as she dropped that bombshell on him. "You have a daughter?'

Flame nodded. "Selena, and before you ask, no, the dad isn't on the scene. We've been living with my mum."

"You did all this to give your daughter a better life." David reiterated what she'd told him, trying to come to terms with the fact that he'd been dating a single mum. If he'd known that from the beginning, he'd have run a mile.

"I'm with you because I like you, David. Don't worry. I'd never expect, or want, you to play daddy to my daughter. You're far too selfish." Her laugh cut him deep, only because he knew it was true. He was no role model for a child and not any more reliable than his own parents.

"That takes me back to my original point. I don't think we have a future together."

"Okay, but can we talk about it later? Let me get this premiere over with first."

Stunned by the revelations tonight, he agreed to put the big talk on hold until they had time and privacy for a proper conversation.

"The rain's getting heavier out there." Flame sounded far away as he pondered over these past months together and the reasons behind them, none of which were particularly flattering.

His other shiny red status symbol picked up speed as he pushed down on the accelerator, keen to get tonight's charade over with as soon as possible.

The city lights streaked by until he felt as though he were flying. Then he was.

"Look out!"

Flame's shout came too late. The car skidded across the greasy road, leaving him powerless as they hurtled towards the steel barriers edging the hard shoulder.

The windscreen shattered around him and the deployed air bag buffeted his body.

The last sound he heard was the ticking of the engine punctuating the eerie silence. Then the world around him descended into blackness.

* * * *

It took a while for David's eyes to adjust. When he first opened them, he'd feared he'd gone blind. Then he remembered the sound of the tyres screeching as he'd tried to regain control of the car and the pungent smell of burning rubber. They'd crashed. The lights had been smashed when they'd hit the barrier.

He didn't know how they'd got out, but at least he didn't appear to be hurt. Unless he was suffering from delayed shock, he couldn't feel any pain. There was no sign of Flame to see if the same could be said for her.

There was some rustling nearby and he remembered they were down in a ditch at the side of the motorway. *Oh God.* He'd read that people were never more than a few feet away from rats in the city, and he couldn't handle vermin being around him. He had to get out of there.

"Hello?" There had to be someone out there, hopefully with a torch so he could see where he was going.

"W-who's there?" A shaky female voice sounded in the shadows a second before he heard the flick of a switch and a bright light blinded him.

"It's David. Who am I talking to? Where the hell am I?" He lifted his hand to shield his eyes from the light and squinted at the source of the voice, which certainly didn't sound like Flame.

There was a high-pitched squeal and some shuffling from what he now could see was a bed. *I'm in someone's bedroom? How the hell did I end up here?* It wasn't anywhere he recognised. This was smaller than his en suite bathroom, for goodness' sake. The clothes and rubbish strewn over the floor made it look like more of a squat compared to the five-star opulence of the residences he usually frequented.

"If it's drug money you're after, I don't have any. The café's not mine. There's nothing worth stealing here."

"I can see that." A glance around the room told him there was nothing of value there—unless one counted the old TV-DVD combo perched on a cheap white melamine chest of drawers or the cage in the corner where some furry creature was trying to gnaw its way through the bars. When he compared it to his bedroom—or even one of his spare rooms—he felt as though he should be donating something to this charitable cause.

"Keep away from me or I'll phone the police." The puffy-eyed, red-nosed creature with mad bed hair gradually rose from its pit. David held his hands up in surrender, afraid to spook her any more than he already had. Besides, it was one thing courting publicity for his own benefit, but if the press got wind of him breaking and entering some random house, his business would suffer along with his reputation.

"Pardon me for the inconvenience, madam. I don't know what I'm doing here either. I'll leave now. There's no need to get the police involved." He backed up and reached for the door handle. Instead of it turning in his hand, he seemed to miss his mark altogether.

Strange. Perhaps the accident had somehow affected his hand-to-eye co-ordination. He tried again. To his horror, he watched his fingers swipe through the metal handle as though it was nothing more than a figment of his imagination.

"Get out!"

He turned back to see the squat-dweller lob a box of tissues at his head. With no time to duck out of the way, he closed his eyes and braced himself for the inevitable hit. Except the anticipated pointy-edged box stabbing him in the eyeball was replaced with that strange whooshing sensation again. The box slammed into the door and slid to the floor as though he wasn't standing there at all. There was another scream, followed by a string of projectiles launched in his direction. A book, an alarm clock and a phone—which he knew she'd come to regret—hit the wooden panelling behind him in quick succession before creating a small pile of bewilderment on the threadbare carpet.

Another shriek.

"Please, will you stop that incessant screaming? You're giving me a headache."

Strictly speaking, he couldn't feel anything—not even his heart pounding in his chest or his pulse throbbing in his veins, which he would've expected in such strange circumstances.

Nothing. It was disconcerting, to say the least.

Still, the high-pitched squealing was getting on his nerves, and he'd prefer she stopped so he could think straight and figure out what was going on.

"W-what are you?" Not *who*, he noted but *what*, which was an odd term to use when he was obviously a man—a rich, handsome, successful man who'd never been thrown out of a woman's bedroom in his life.

She hugged the knees of her ridiculous nightwear tighter, although there was no need for her to be afraid. He had no intention of going anywhere near her and he'd be out of there as soon as he worked out how.

There was a chance he'd catch something if he stayed much longer.

"I'm afraid I have no more clue than you do as to how, or why, I'm here, and I certainly no desire to stay a second longer but, as you can see, I appear to be having a problem with that." His efforts to open the door again produced the same futile result. He even tried putting his foot through it, to no avail. Every attempt at physical contact resulted in him swinging at thin air.

"A little help might get rid of me quicker." If sarcasm could unlock doors, the whole world would be open to him right now.

The wary warden of his current prison cell climbed slowly from the bed and padded towards him. She stopped just short of the door, waiting for him to stand aside, away from her, before she opened it.

Hallelujah!

The prison gate swung open, enabling him to follow his liberator out through the flat towards the front door, the rest of which was no more glamorous than the main bedroom. Plain painted walls were devoid of any pictures or art, and the whole apartment was so small that it was claustrophobic.

He had no clue what was waiting for him outside, but it had to be better than being locked in this bizarre new territory, frightening in its austerity, with a strange woman—a very strange woman, who was breathing her own sigh of relief as she opened the front door for her uninvited guest to leave.

Except David hit some sort of invisible wall every time he tried to step outside the apartment.

"What on earth?" He lost the very last thread of his patience as he tried and failed to shoulder-charge his way through the invisi-shield.

The worst bit was that whenever his new friend tried to shove him out, she fell right through him and landed in a heap on the landing, looking up at him with complete bewilderment. He couldn't even help her up and had to watch her gather what little there was left of her fleecy dignity and get to her feet.

"What the fuck?" She echoed his bewilderment with more colourful language than he'd have preferred, but with exactly the same pitch of horror and desire to break out of this nightmare as he had.

They stood staring at each other, wide-eyed and open-mouthed, until she slowly extended a finger and attempted to prod him. Instead of skin touching skin, her digit gradually disappeared into his arm. She withdrew her hand, only to jab it again into his other arm.

"Will you please stop poking me? I'm not some sort of sideshow at the circus." He didn't know what he was in his current state.

"Can you feel it?" She did it again, her forehead furrowed with concentrated effort.

"No, but it's not very nice having a complete stranger prod me as though I'm some sort of unidentified object."

"Technically, that's exactly what you are, and, for your information, it's not very nice having a complete stranger turn up in your flat who you can't get rid of, either." She folded her arms and tilted her chin into the air. At least she was no longer looking at him as a threat—more of a household pest, now that they knew he had no physical presence. It was a fact which wasn't as comforting to him as it seemed to be to her.

"Good point, but apparently we're both stuck with me being here until we figure this thing out." He followed her back inside the apartment with a heavy heart.

"Right. We need to think of a logical explanation." She paced the small living room, hands on her hips, clearly trying to accept this was actually happening. Then she rolled up her sleeve and pinched the skin of her forearm between her thumb and finger.

"I'm still here. It's real, I'm afraid." He smiled and waved to prove he wasn't the product of her imagination she hoped he was.

"Okay. Okay. What's the last thing you remember?" Stroppy, ploddy lady stopped walking around in circles long enough to question him.

That image of the windscreen wipers and the blurred city lights popped into his head.

"I was driving... It was dark...raining. I think I crashed." That dizzying sensation had his head spinning again, only this time it came with the significance of the memory.

The woman slapped her hand over her mouth. "Oh God, I think you might be dead!"

About the Author

Claudia Ambrose has been in love with words her whole life. She's been writing for nearly as long. *Build You Up* is her debut novel. She lives in a small house in Virginia with her husband and far too many cats.

Claudia loves to hear from readers. You can find her contact information, website details and author profile page at https://www.firstforromance.com

ENTWINED PUBLISHING

www.ingramcontent.com/pod-product-compliance
Lightning Source LLC
Chambersburg PA
CBHW020818260626
47169CB00003B/716